Trudie's Tears
Book Six in Clover Creek Caravan
Kirsten Osbourne

Chapter One

Thursday, June 11th, 1852

I know I shouldn't be happy for the short respite we've had from traveling, but I am. I'm not happy the former captain is so ill, of course, but I am happy that we were able to stay in place and the men had time to hunt. I am able to cook venison for our supper tonight, and I've been able to dry a great deal more for future meals. It's good because my meat supply was running low. Even I can't eat bacon for every meal.

I have enjoyed having other people join me at my fire for supper every night. Emily fills the silence that seems to permeate the air between her father and me. Neither of us ask questions of the other, which makes the quiet almost deafening. Thank heaven for Emily.

I don't look forward to driving again tomorrow, but I do look forward to being somewhere I can hide—two thousand miles from home, or thereabouts. It will be good for me to lose myself in a new life and forget what has transpired. Forget why I'm on this godforsaken trail.

We are almost to Independence Rock from what I'm told, and that is the halfway point of our journey. I've been told the goal is to be there by July fourth, and we will make it weeks before that date. Perhaps our journey will be easier than that of some of the others because of the time of year we left. At the beginning of the journey the oxen had trouble finding good grass to graze on because the snow had melted so recently. Now, though...the journey is much easier than it would have been if we'd left later.

I thank God every day that I've made it this far with no one being suspicious of me. If I can just make it to Oregon, I will again change my name and lose myself among the immigrants.

Trudie knelt by her fire, making a meal for both herself and a father and daughter she'd met along the trail. It was a better meal than she could usually make because Mr. Simmons had brought her some meat. They'd been camped in the same place for three days, but they'd be moving on the next day. Finally. Trudie wasn't certain why everyone was pretending to care if the former captain of their company—George Bedwell—lived or died.

It was strange the way the people in their group had formed almost a family, and Trudie was the red-headed stepchild of the family. She didn't mind though. If she got close to people there was a danger of her sharing her secret, and that would never do. People around her didn't need to know she'd...well, she couldn't even complete the thought. She was too afraid of being caught.

The venison roast she'd made that evening would taste delicious with the potatoes, carrots, and fresh bread she'd also made. It would be hard to return to eating the simpler meals every evening. As an unmarried woman traveling the treacherous trail to Oregon, she was driving all day, and when it came to cooking meals in the evening, she had little energy to make them happen. She hoped having two extra people to cook for would make her care more about what she ate, but they hadn't really moved at all in the time since she'd agreed to cook for Mr. Simmons and little Emily—save for crossing the North Platte River.

Emily was a dear. There was just something about the child that made Trudie smile, and she was happy to have her there every evening for supper. It was nice to be able to be with others and not constantly on her own. Oh, she was sure others would have become friends with her if she hadn't been so prickly. She knew that others had tried, but it was so much safer to keep them *all* at arm's distance.

She'd formed a tentative friendship with Penelope, but that was only because Penelope had agreed to never ask questions about her past. It worked well for them.

Trudie had just finished the gravy for their supper when she noticed Mr. Simmons and little Emily walking toward her campfire. She wanted to jump up and welcome her guests as she would have before...well, just before. But she couldn't. She had to make sure everyone knew she was quiet and didn't say much to others.

Mr. Simmons stopped at the fire. "Is there anything I can help you with, Miss Brown?"

Trudie shook her head. "No, thank you. Everything is ready." She smiled at Emily, feeling more comfortable talking to the child than she did anyone else in their wagon train. "How was your day, Emily?"

Emily smiled. "It was fun. I got to play with the others today. We were playing by the river and jumping on rocks."

"You be careful by the river," Trudie said automatically. It was due to a child falling into the river that the former captain was so ill. He'd almost drowned saving a young widow's daughter, and they certainly didn't need to lose anyone else on this awful journey.

"Yes, ma'am. I will!" Emily plopped down on the ground. "Supper smells delicious."

"I'm sure it will be, thanks to your father bringing me some venison today. I wasn't sure what I was going to cook." Trudie didn't look at Mr. Simmons as she spoke. She didn't want to invite friendship even with him, though she was cooking for his family.

"Don't most of the women share meat?" Mr. Simmons asked.

Trudie nodded. "Most do. I can't really contribute so I don't take anything away from the others. I have lots of jerky." She didn't want to admit to him that it was because she was antisocial that no one shared with her. She dished up plates for them all and offered Mr. Simmons his first, and then gave a plate to Emily.

"I love to eat your food, Miss Brown," Emily said. "You're the best cook in the whole wide world!"

Trudie laughed, feeling joy when she was with this child. "I'm not so sure about that. I hear Margaret Prewitt is a *much* better cook than me."

Emily seemed to consider the question as Trudie put her own plate on her lap. "No, I think you're better, but don't tell Amanda or Sally!"

Trudie smiled. "I won't tell anyone." Truthfully, though, she should be the best cook in camp. She'd been trained to be a professional cook from childhood by her mother, who had cooked for a wealthy family in New York. Her parents had been Irish immigrants, and her father had died shortly after coming to America. She looked at Mr. Simmons. "Would you mind saying a blessing over our meal, Mr. Simmons?"

He nodded, and she immediately bowed her head. His prayer was short and only involved blessing the food and the hands which had prepared it, but he rarely said anything at all around Trudie.

As they ate, Emily regaled them with tales of her day playing with the other children and collecting buffalo chips to be used to cook their meals. "I don't like having to pick up the buffalo chips, but I like eating, so I have to do my part," Emily said with a shrug. "All of the children have to help. Even the really little ones!"

At that, Trudie looked at Mr. Simmons. "There's certainly enough food here that I can save it for our noon meal tomorrow if you'd like."

He nodded. "We'll be driving again tomorrow. May I hitch up your team for you in the morning, so you have more time to deal with our breakfast?" he offered.

"That would be most welcome. Thank you." Trudie didn't mind cooking, but driving and dealing with her livestock had proven difficult for her. She was strong from a lifetime of hard work, but her work had always been done indoors.

"Can we have johnny cakes tomorrow morning?" Emily asked. "Papa and I have honey we can put on them."

Trudie wasn't sure that Emily should be offering her family's honey for breakfast for the three of them, but Mr. Simmons simply nodded. "We'd be happy to share the honey we have. Emily's mother had a sweet tooth, and I'm afraid she purchased more honey than we could possibly use on this trip."

It was the first time he'd mentioned his wife to her, and Trudie wanted to ask questions, but she wouldn't answer them, so she had no right to ask. "I'll gladly use some for all of us," Trudie said.

Mr. Simmons finished his meal. "Emily, help Miss Brown with the dishes, and then come back to our camp."

"Yes, Papa." Emily immediately got to her feet and collected the dishes her father had used.

As Mr. Simmons walked away, Trudie broke her own most important rule by asking the child a question. "Do you miss your mama?"

Emily looked sad for a moment. "I do, but I know she's in heaven with Jesus, and that makes it easier to not cry much."

"So, we're doing johnny cakes for breakfast," Trudie said enthusiastically. "Do you want bacon with them?"

"Yes, please! I love bacon."

"Me too," Trudie confided. "It's my favorite meat." She was glad the bacon would last because the other meats they had to choose from weren't nearly as tasty. She'd brought two pigs with her to start raising them when they reached Oregon. She couldn't wait to get there. She'd already changed her name once, and when they reached Oregon, she'd change it again. Hopefully, no one would be able to find her. Hopefully, no one was searching for her, but she couldn't risk her life by counting on that.

She and Emily chatted while they worked on doing the dishes and putting them away. "I wish I could stay here with you tonight," Emily said.

"Stay with me?" Trudie was surprised. "You don't want to stay with your papa?"

Emily shrugged. "I love my papa, but he's sad. I'd rather not have to be with someone so sad all the time."

"Of course, he's sad," Trudie said softly. "He lost his wife."

"She didn't *want* to go to Oregon," Emily said. "She told papa it would be too hard, but he said she had to go."

Trudie wasn't surprised. Few women wanted to go west. The men thought it was a great adventure, but the woman saw it for what it was. More work with fewer friends about. "Most women don't want to go to Oregon."

"But you do. You don't have a husband telling you what to do?" Emily asked.

Trudie smiled at Emily's wording. "I don't. I never found just the right man."

"Maybe my papa is the right man," Emily said as they put the last of the dishes away. "You both want to go to Oregon."

"I'm not so sure about that, Emily."

Emily shrugged, spontaneously hugging Trudie. "See you in the morning, and I won't forget the honey!" With that, the girl turned and ran across the circle of the wagons to where her father was camped.

Trudie watched her until she knew she was with her father, and then she sat down, closing her eyes and wishing for a dreamless night. She mended her dress by the light of the fire until most of the camp was settled for the night.

And then she got out her bedroll and climbed under her wagon. Closing her eyes, she prayed for a quiet night. A calm night. A night when she wouldn't wake up terrified.

TRUDIE WOKE A FEW SHORT hours later, sweating profusely. It wasn't that it was too hot. It was downright cold during the night. No, that wasn't the problem at all. She sat up and rubbed her hands over her face, reminding herself that she was safe now. "No one can find you. You changed your name. You're safe." The words were the same ones she whispered to herself every time she woke from one of her nightmares. Nightmares that were filled with policemen with guns. With a hangman's noose. With a jail filled with terrible people.

Instead of trying to go back to sleep—Trudie knew the effort would be futile—she got up and folded her bedroll neatly, starting her morning fire. Some families had cold breakfasts in the morning, but she preferred to have something warm in her belly to start her day. The days on the trail were long and difficult. She had to be as ready for them as she could possibly be.

After putting the coffee pot on the fire, she deftly mixed up the batter for the johnny cakes, and then she made a pan of cornbread. It would go nicely with their lunch, and there would be enough left for supper. She thought about her provisions and decided to just do a jerky gravy over biscuits for breakfast the following morning. It wouldn't be the best meal in the world, but at least it wouldn't be beans.

When Emily and Mr. Simmons joined her, she had their breakfast ready and the bacon had been cooked to a perfect crisp. Emily took her plate and handed Trudie the honey. "I need lots of honey, please."

Trudie smiled. "I can do lots of honey." She poured more than she would have put on her own johnny cakes and turned to Mr. Simmons. "Would you like me to pour for you?"

He shook his head. "I don't eat honey on my johnny cakes."

"I see." Trudie poured honey onto her own and put the stopper back into the jug of honey. "Thank you for sharing your supply then."

"Keep it. We're eating here anyway," he said.

Trudie thought it was an odd situation they had. They met three times a day for meals, and he prayed for them three times per day. He would hitch up her wagon, and she would cook. He brought her meat when he had it. Other than that, they said little to each other.

Emily happily ate her breakfast, smiling throughout the entire meal. "We get to move again today!"

"Is there any news on the former captain?" Trudie asked.

Mr. Simmons nodded. "He woke up yesterday morning. The doctor thinks he's going to be all right, but he'll have to ride for a good long while. He's not strong enough to try and drive. One of his sons is going to drive for them."

"I see. We can't wait any longer?"

"No, we can't. We've been camped for too long already. It's time for us to move on."

Trudie nodded. She had to wonder if they'd wait longer if it was someone else who had fallen ill the way the former captain had, but she knew better. There was no time to wait for anyone. They had to get to Oregon before it was too cold, and there was only one way to do that. Constant movement.

Trudie tried to enjoy the drive that morning, but her dreams still haunted her. She could see *him* fall down the stairs, and she could hear the screams of one of the maids as she discovered him.

Trudie had grabbed some jewelry to sell, and she'd run. She had no idea if anyone was following her, but her mind played tricks on her, and she saw policeman's uniforms off in the horizon constantly.

The river was calming. The oxen plodded along with their usual slow pace which allowed for the women and children to keep up by walking along beside or behind the wagons. She thought about what her name should be when she got to Oregon.

She'd been born Gertrude O'Keefe, but Trudie Brown sounded so much more "American" to her. She was proud of her Irish heritage, but she couldn't let her Irish flag wave. She wasn't safe. Her mother had called her Trudie when she was a girl, so it was easy to take the nickname on the drive. But what would she call herself when she got to Oregon? There were so many names to choose from.

When they stopped for the noon meal, her mind was still on what she would call herself when they arrived, but she did her best to get the food out and served for her two guests. She'd agreed to cook for three because she couldn't bear to cook for one for another minute. She thought she might open a small café or even a bakery when they arrived, but she wasn't sure if that would bring too much attention to herself. Was she a wanted woman? Or had the authorities forgotten about her?

Emily was as enthusiastic as always as they ate their noon meal, and Trudie was happy to just listen to the girl, not trying to make conversation herself. They'd seen a butterfly she'd never seen before while walking that morning, and the children had all tried to catch it. The only way Emily was really able to describe it was beautiful, but that was good enough as far as Trudie was concerned.

At the end of the meal, Emily stayed to help with the dishes, and then she went off to rest with the other children as they got ready for their afternoon trek.

Trudie was glad to see her go. She loved the child, but she was lost in her own thoughts.

She was thankful not to have to unhitch the oxen and hitch a new team everyday at noon now. It was good that Mr. Simmons had taken that chore from her, though she questioned if she should allow herself to rely on *anyone*.

By that evening, when she was in front of a campfire and cooking once again, she'd almost driven herself crazy looking for uniformed men behind every rock and every wave of the prairie grasses. She was thankful to have someone to cook for, but she realized the worst part of this journey for her was the time alone with her thoughts as she drove.

Every time she closed her eyes, she could see Mr. Baldwin falling to his death. She could see the odd angle of his neck as he lay dead. She could hear the screams that filled the house.

When she wasn't driving, it was easier to concentrate on other things. Would the Simmons be happy with the meal she made? Should she perhaps make a dessert using the honey they'd provided? Had Emily or one of the other children captured the elusive butterfly?

They were halfway through their evening meal when Emily said something that shocked Trudie through and through. "I think you two should get married. Then I'd have a mama to walk with me and a papa to drive. No one would have to sew for us or cook for us."

Trudie choked on her biscuit. "I don't know about that, Emily. People need to be in love to get married."

"You could be married without loving each other," Emily said. "I just need you both, and it would be easier. Don't you think?"

Mr. Simmons frowned. "That's enough, Emily. I'll talk to Miss Brown about it after supper, but you are not to mention it again. Do you hear me?"

Emily sighed dramatically. "Yes, Papa."

Trudie was shocked to hear that Mr. Simmons was planning to talk to her about marriage, but she was certain he'd simply tell her to not mind Emily. What else could he do? The man was definitely in mourning and had no desire to remarry.

After the meal, Mr. Simmons got to his feet. "Emily, you help Miss Brown wash up, and then I want you to go play with Amanda and Sally. Miss Brown, if you'll join me at my wagon after the washing up is done, I'd like to take you for a nice long walk so we can talk."

Trudie nodded. "I'll be there." She wouldn't marry him, of course, but she'd be there. How could a wanted woman who planned to change her name again marry a man on the Oregon Trail? No, it couldn't happen, but he wouldn't want it to anyway. Emily could want it all day, and it just wouldn't happen.

As they washed the dishes together, Emily was as happy as ever, singing as she wiped the dishes dry. Trudie's mind was on her fear of being alone with a man. Surely, he wouldn't hurt her though. She'd just have to make certain to stay within earshot of camp.

Chapter Two

Thursday, June 11th, 1852

With Emily's prodding, I've decided to ask Miss Brown to be my wife. It's odd, but I don't even know her first name, and I'm going to propose. I don't really want another wife, as I'm still heartbroken about losing the one I had, but Emily is right in that she does need a mother.

I hope to make the argument that Miss Brown's ife will be easier if I drive and she can walk with the other women. And I know she cares for Emily already. I can see it every time I see her glance at my daughter. It makes a lot of sense for me to marry her, though it won't be a physical marriage at all. I'm not ready for that yet. How could I be? I killed the love of my life. Another love is not a good idea at this time.

We moved on today as planned. The captain has healed enough that he is at least awake and able to eat and drink. I'm still not sure why we paused the train when he became ill when he wouldn't wait for a woman to give birth. I suppose the new captains are better at forgiving than I am. I just wish I could forgive myself.

Trudie was nervous about the walk she was taking with Mr. Simmons, worried he would talk to her about marrying him. She knew it was what Emily wanted, but she also knew Emily simply wanted to have a mother again. That was no reason to marry. Besides, she couldn't ask a man to live with her past. No one should have to be saddled with her mistake.

Trudie walked with Emily to the wagon where Mr. Simmons was waiting for her. "Are you ready to walk, Miss Brown?"

Trudie nodded. "Yes, of course, I am." She smoothed the front of her dress nervously. Not only had she never been married, she'd never even been courted. Walking alone with a man was difficult. Especially after her experience with... She couldn't even think his name without shuddering.

Mr. Simmons looked down at Emily. "You go play with Mrs. Prewitt's girls. I've already talked to Mrs. Prewitt, and she'll watch out for you."

Emily nodded. "Yes, Papa." She ran toward the spot where Amanda and Sally were playing with little Annie, who was Betty's adopted daughter.

Thinking about Betty sent a pang of guilt through Trudie. She'd been downright rude to the other woman, not wanting to get too close to anyone. The questions people asked bothered her because she hated to lie, and she couldn't answer them honestly.

As she and Mr. Simmons headed toward the open prairie outside of the protective circle of wagons, Trudie looked around. She was surprised at how indelibly the wagons had marked the trail. There were ruts in the ground that each wagon drove over. Even this early in the year, there was little grass left between the wheels. The different wagon trains were hard on the land. She couldn't help but wonder if some of those ruts would still be there in fifty years. Or even one or two hundred years.

"I'm sure you're wondering why I asked you to walk with me today," Mr. Simmons said softly.

Trudie nodded. "Yes, I am."

"Emily has been hounding me to marry you for days now. I am not ready to be in love again, but I do think Emily would be more settled, and life would be easier if I had a wife."

Trudie immediately started shaking her head. "I don't think that's a good idea."

"Hear me out." He stopped walking and held up a hand. "Your life would be made easier by this. You would be able to walk with the other women and not drive any longer. You would simply be responsible for meals, laundry, and the things all the women are responsible for. You wouldn't be required to drive at all or help in any way the other women don't."

Trudie frowned. "There are things you don't know about me." She wouldn't tell him though. He'd never look at her the same way again, and she had no idea if he would leave her in the next town they passed. It was best if no one knew, but that meant no real relationships could be formed.

"And things you don't know about me. We will respect one another and not ask questions we wouldn't want to answer." It didn't seem to bother him that he had no idea about her past.

She bit her lip. "I don't know if someone will be coming after me. I've done some things on the wrong side of the law."

He shrugged. "I've done many things I'm not proud of. I won't ask questions if you don't."

Trudie looked at him, her eyes narrowed. "You wouldn't require anything physical from me?"

"Just the things I've mentioned. There will be no need for us to share a bed. I miss my wife and love her a great deal still. I don't want a physical marriage. I just need someone to help me get to Oregon. And you've shown Emily and me a great deal of kindness."

"Are you certain you don't want to find someone else?"

He gave a short laugh that didn't sound amused at all. "Where do you think I can find someone? You realize we're in the middle of the prairie, don't you? How am I supposed to find someone to marry?"

"I suppose you're right." Trudie liked the idea of having a closer relationship with little Emily, but she wasn't certain how she felt about marrying the girl's father. She still had a hard time being in close proximity to a man after what had happened. "May I take some time to think about it?"

He nodded. "Absolutely. Will twenty-four hours be enough? Or do you need to wait until Saturday night?"

"I'll make a decision by this time tomorrow if you'd like to walk again to discuss it. I don't want to get Emily's hopes up by discussing anything in front of her." She was pretty certain her answer would be no, but thinking about it would be wise. It would make her life easier in the short term.

"I think that's wise. Emily thinks a great deal of you, and whether you're on the wrong side of the law or not, I believe that you won't do anything to hurt her. That's important to me."

"And if I decide I no longer want to be married to you once we reach Oregon?"

"Then we shall pretend the wedding never happened. No one will remember us from our time on the trail. We'll simply make sure to settle away from the others."

"Did you know everyone plans to settle together?" she asked.

Mr. Simmons shook his head. "I didn't know that, but I'm not surprised. With Emily and I being on our own, no one would really talk to us about that."

"I can understand that. I haven't been invited to live near the others, but they all talk about it openly."

"Do you want to settle close to them?"

She sighed. "I will probably change my name again when I get out west, so no, I don't think I do. It would be easier to be found that way."

"Do you really fear someone chasing you?"

She nodded. "I fear it. It may be an unrealistic fear, but I can't get it out of my head."

"I see." He turned and began walking back toward camp. "I can't see you doing anything to hurt another, so whatever you did, couldn't be as bad as you make it sound."

"It's just as bad as I make it sound. I don't want you to lessen it in your head." Trudie couldn't let him believe it was something minor, like stealing a loaf of bread.

Mr. Simmons sighed. "I won't be asking questions about it."

"That's good. I won't be answering any."

"Well, I appreciate your honesty, Miss Brown."

"If we're considering marriage, you should call me Trudie."

"And you should call me Joseph."

Trudie nodded. "Joseph it shall be."

As soon as they were back within the circle of the wagons, she rushed off to her own campsite. She didn't want people to see them together and assume they were getting married. No, the decision needed to lie squarely with her, and have nothing to do with gossip.

Dare she grab a bit of happiness where she could? Marrying Joseph would mean nothing to her but being Emily's mother...that was something that would bring her true joy.

Perhaps she could consider it. Perhaps.

Trudie thought of little else during the next day. She went through the motions of cooking and driving, but her mind was on whether or not it would be smart of her to marry Joseph. Surely, there were much smarter things she could do, but would marrying him be so wrong?

She already loved his daughter. And being married, which would require a name change, would help protect her. She would no longer be a woman traveling alone. Instead, she'd be a part of a family. If there were men hunting her, surely they'd be looking for a woman alone, and not a family. Perhaps it was a smart way to hide within the wagon train.

When it was time for her to walk with Joseph again that evening, Trudie had not yet made up her mind about what she should do. She hated the idea of saddling Emily and Joseph with a wanted woman, but she also knew it would make her safer.

They walked in silence for a short while, and then he turned to her. "Have you had sufficient time to make your decision?" he asked softly.

Until that very moment, Trudie hadn't known what her answer would be. "Yes, I'll marry you. But you must never question me about what brought me onto the trail." It would be the only way they could work well together.

He shrugged. "I find I'm not overly curious. I just want someone who will help care for my child."

"I will do that." Trudie wondered if she should explain, but why put him in danger? No man would want to be in a position where he had to choose between protecting his wife and upholding the law.

"We could marry tomorrow evening?" he suggested. "After the drive, but before the dancing. That way you'll have time to move your supplies to my wagon before we start out again on Monday."

"I do have several oxen. I have four pair, which can of course add to your supply."

"That is more than we will need. I have four pair myself. We don't need eight pair of oxen." He frowned. "I suppose I can use whichever of the cattle make it all the way to Oregon to start my herd."

"Your herd? Do you plan to be a dairy farmer or a rancher?" she asked. She hadn't thought to question him about his intentions once they arrived.

"I will be a rancher. The life is difficult, but very rewarding. I will be able to provide well for a family."

She nodded. "I see. I had thought about opening a small café." But she would change her name first and make certain no one knew her.

"You could do that if you wished." He started walking back toward the camp. "Would it be just a café or possibly a boarding house?"

She shuddered. "Boarding houses are usually for men, especially out west. I fear I wouldn't be able to be alone with men without fear."

He frowned at her. "Have you always feared men?"

"Just for a short while. I will get over it."

"I do hope so. I could see you doing very well with a boarding house. A café seems like it would be geared more toward women than men, and there are more bachelors than women in the west."

"That's true. I'll think about it." And she would. Perhaps if they decided to stay married a boarding house would work. She had no desire to be alone around men, but if she was married, it would make things easier for her. She would be protected, and the men would understand that when they called her Mrs. Simmons.

"When we return to camp, I'll talk to the preacher and tell him we want to marry after supper tomorrow. Would you like to be the one to tell Emily?"

"You wouldn't mind?" Trudie hadn't dreamed he would allow her to share the news with his daughter. She couldn't wait to see the child's face.

"I wouldn't mind at all. The two of you have a good relationship, and I want that to continue for as long as it can. Emily needs a stepmother who is kind to her. I hope you will continue to be kind."

"I would never be unkind to a child. The only times I have been unkind were to hide my past." She'd almost said she'd never be unkind to anyone, but it wasn't true. She hadn't been overly kind to Betty or any of the other women who had tried to talk to her about her past.

"If you ever want to tell me, you may. I will not pry." He stopped walking for a moment and looked over at her. "I do expect the same courtesy. I will talk about most anything, but not my late wife. That subject is off-limits."

"I will endeavor to keep that in mind," Trudie said. She understood. There were many reasons for traveling west, and she wouldn't question his reasons for anything if he didn't question hers. She had to wonder why he wouldn't speak about his wife though. There must be something there no one knew about.

Once they were back in camp, she found Emily playing with her friends and called her over. Squatting down, Trudie said softly, "Your papa and I are to be married tomorrow after supper."

Emily clasped her hands in front of her, her face excited. "I shall be the best daughter you ever dreamed of having."

Trudie smiled. "I'm certain you shall." As she headed back to her camp, Trudie had a smile on her face. The excitement the little girl had displayed made her feel good about the marriage. Maybe she'd later regret it, but she would make Emily happy now. And for some reason, making Emily happy had become something she wanted to strive for.

As Trudie fell asleep that night, she felt at peace for the first time since leaving New York City.

PUSHED UP AGAINST A wall in the darkened corridor of the manor home where she worked, Gertrude tried to scream, but her attacker's hand over her mouth prevented her from making a sound. She struggled, wanting her employer to remember he was married with small children.

Yes, his wife was out for the day, but that shouldn't matter to his marriage vows.

Gertrude bit the hand covering her mouth, and Mr. Baldwin let out a yelp of pain. He glowered at her, slapping her so hard she fell to the floor at his feet. Gertrude struggled to get to her feet again, and he once again pinned her to the wall. "You're going to be quiet and let me have my fun."

"No, I won't!" Gertrude screamed at the top of her lungs, hoping against hope someone would come to help her. She knew some of the maids had suffered Mr. Baldwin's advances, but she hadn't been so unlucky until that day. She doubted anyone would come. Everyone knew what was happening and no one ever raised a finger to stop him.

Gertrude knew she was truly on her own in a way she never had been before. Her mother had died two short months before, and now she was being attacked by her employer. She felt as if her mother was frowning down at her from heaven, saddened by what was happening.

Gertrude began to kick and pound him with her fists, and he just laughed at her. Stopping fighting for just a moment to gather her strength to get the man off her, she pushed as hard as she could, planning to turn and run as soon as possible.

But there was no point in turning away. Mr. Baldwin hit the banister and lost his balance, toppling over the edge of the balcony. He landed on his back on the floor below, his neck at an odd angle. One of the maids below screamed upon seeing him, and Gertrude was certain the maid saw it was her who had pushed him.

She ran. She didn't know what else to do. Making a quick stop in the master bedroom, she went to Mrs. Baldwin's jewelry box and grabbed two rings and a necklace. She was now a murderer. What did it matter if she added stealing to her crimes?

As she ran down the stairs with the jewelry clutched in her hand, she passed the man she'd killed, expecting him to grab her ankle and pull her to the floor at any second. And then he did.

He pulled her to the floor, and his mouth, which was full of blood, smiled. "You can't get away from me that easily!"

Trudie woke in a cold sweat. The same way she'd woken every night for months. The dream was always the same. Killing Mr. Baldwin over and over was the worst punishment she could think of. Truly, she wasn't sure if prison could be worse.

For once, she'd slept as late as the others in camp, and she heard the women stirring around her. She immediately got up and stoked her campfire. She was always happy when it didn't go out completely overnight, and she could just put more buffalo chips on it to build it up again.

For breakfast, she made eggs and bacon. Several of the families had brought chickens, and they would sell the eggs to those willing to pay. Trudie had more money than many on the trail because she'd stolen more jewelry than she'd needed. Though she hadn't planned to go west when she'd fled from that terrible house, she had thought to living on her own. It was a good thing because she wouldn't have been able to survive so long otherwise.

Once breakfast was ready, Joseph and Emily came to her camp. She poured a cup of coffee for each of them, laughing when Emily made a face. "You know the doctor says that we will live longer if we drink coffee."

"I know. I just hate it!"

"What if I start making you tea with a little honey in it? Could you drink tea?"

Emily nodded emphatically. "I don't like tea, but it's so much better than coffee!"

"I tend to agree," Trudie said with a smile.

Joseph sipped his own coffee. "Let's pray." As usual, his prayer was simple, but it blessed their food, and that's all Trudie was worried about. "The pastor will marry us after supper and before the dancing."

Emily looked like she wanted to squeal with excitement. "It will be like you have a wedding dance. Papa, you will dance with me at your wedding dance?"

He nodded. "Of course, I will."

"And you'll dance with Trudie?"

Joseph looked uncomfortable at the question. "If Trudie wants to dance with me, I'd be more than happy to."

Trudie shrugged. "I'm not sure I'll be up for dancing after driving all day." It would give him a good excuse not to have to dance with her, no matter how Emily felt about it.

Emily sighed. "I would like to see you dance at your wedding, but if Trudie is too tired, then I will understand."

Joseph nodded. "We will see how we all feel this evening."

Emily nodded, devoting herself to the task of eating her breakfast. "We need johnny cakes again tomorrow, Trudie."

Trudie smiled. "I thought you'd like eggs for a change."

"No. I want johnny cakes every morning."

Joseph shook his head. "It's a good think the trail is so much work, or you'd look like a giant white blueberry when we got to Oregon."

Emily giggled and stood up, pulling her skirts out to the sides and rounding her arms. "You would just have more Emily to love, Papa."

He laughed. "And we all need as much Emily as we can get."

Chapter Three

Friday, June 12th, 1852

Mr. Simmons asked me to marry him last night, which surprised me a great deal. His daughter has wanted us to marry for a little while, but he came right out and admitted to me that he still loves his wife. The marriage would be in name only, and I would take on the duty of walking with Emily every day. I already cook for them, so the marriage wouldn't change my life much except I'd have another name change, which would be good, and I'd walk. I'm not sure how I feel about the idea of walking with the other women after the way I've treated a few of them. Hopefully they'll be as forgiving to me as they were to the former captain.

I have not yet made a decision about what I will do. He did agree to ask me no questions about my past at all. That will make things easier for me. I do like the idea of being Emily's mother. Truly, she is the only reason I'm considering the arrangement. Although, it might also protect me from anyone searching for me.

I'll know soon enough what I plan to do. I must give Mr. Simmons my decision tonight when we walk again. For Emily, I want to scream yes. For myself, I want to hide away and never make another decision again.

As she drove that day, Trudie was very aware it was her last day to be driving toward Oregon. Starting on Monday, she would be walking with the other women and the children. It would be strange, but she was excited to do it. She would still need to avoid questions about her past, but she could feel like she belonged since she would be part of a family.

When they stopped that night, she was surprised to see Penelope walking toward her wagon. "Mary killed a buffalo this afternoon. I thought you would like to have a roast to cook for your supper."

"Thank you!" It would be the perfect wedding supper as far as Trudie was concerned. She couldn't slow cook it as she would have liked, but that didn't matter. She'd make stew out of what was left for supper the next day, and that could be cooked slowly over the fire.

"I hear there's going to be a wedding this evening."

"I hear the same thing. I'm not sure I'm doing the right thing, but I'm doing it either way."

Penelope nodded. "I know how you feel. I was the same when I married Herb."

"I'm glad I'm not alone. Tomorrow is going to be interesting deciding what I should take and leaving what I shouldn't." Trudie sighed. "I hate that there's so very much to do."

"I'll help you. It'll be fun. I can even get some of the other ladies to help, if you wouldn't mind people going through your things." Penelope looked solemn as she waited for an answer. Trudie knew the other woman was well aware of her penchant for hiding her past, so it made sense she didn't know which Trudie would choose.

"There's nothing hidden among my things that would bother me if someone saw them." Trudie shrugged. "I left the past back east." She preferred not to even say where she'd lived. It may be silly, but she didn't want anyone knowing she'd killed, deliberately or not.

"Well, then I'll get a group together to help you. We'll have fun doing it." Penelope smiled. "And I'll be there for your wedding. You should get Margaret to fix you a bath. She usually charges, but she tends to give the women who marry a free bath on their wedding day."

Trudie bit her lip. The idea of a bath was appealing, but it would be a busy evening without a bath. She didn't want the other woman to have to haul water just before the dance. "I may take one tomorrow, but there's too much to do this evening. I have to cook this meat for starters." She held up the small pot Penelope had brought the meat in. "Let me get this into my cook pot, and then I'll give yours back."

Penelope nodded. "That sounds good. I'll let Margaret know you'd like to bathe tomorrow."

"I'll do it myself in a bit." Trudie transferred the meat and added some of her rainwater she'd caught for drinking. She was determined to make the meat as appetizing as she could in the short hours it would be before supper. "Thank you so much for thinking of me."

Penelope smiled. "It's our job as women to look out for each other." She accepted the empty pot and walked back toward her wagon.

Trudie got the meat started and walked toward Mrs. Gabriel's wagon. Her friend's words had inspired her to do something she'd never considered doing. "I thought I'd spell you for a bit while everyone goes to church tomorrow. It might be nice for you to be able to go to the service with your children." It was the first overture of friendship Trudie had made toward any of the other women, and though it was hard for her, she could easily sit with the former captain while Mrs. Gabriel went to church.

Mrs. Gabriel smiled. "I would enjoy that immensely if you really don't mind."

"I don't mind," Trudie said. She'd lost a little faith with everything that had happened. She'd been raised to be a strong Christian woman, but she felt as if God had forsaken her when he'd allowed her former employer to try to rape her. She'd prayed every day she would be safe from the man, and she had no idea why God would allow her to be put into such a situation.

"Then I'd appreciate it."

"I'll come after lunch so you can get the children ready if you so choose." Trudie didn't understand the need the others had of dressing in their best for a dance or for Sunday church. They were in the middle of the prairie, and they wouldn't run into many people. Surely it would be better if they simply wore their everyday clothes instead of ruining their best.

"Thank you. There's not much to do with Mr. Bedwell at this point, but he will need someone to give him sips of water when he's ready. I'll have a loaf of bread baked up, and he'll need to eat when he's hungry, but he can only take tiny bites at a time."

"I think I can handle that." Trudie smiled to herself as she walked back toward her own wagon and the cooking roast. In her past, she'd spent time sitting with the sick and helping others as a matter of course. Now, though. Well, maybe she could go back to being the woman she'd once been.

She peeled potatoes and carrots and put them into the pot with the roast. She hated how long a meal like this took on a traveling day, but they had a few hours before the dancing started. Rarely did they dance before eight, and it was just past four. She could get the meal done, they could eat, and dishes could be done in time to marry. She hoped.

She had just finished wiping her hands on her apron when she noticed little Emily skipping toward her. "Hi, Miss Brown!"

"Well, hello there!" Trudie smiled at the girl, thrilled to know she would be her own stepdaughter later that night. "Are you having fun?"

Emily nodded. "Papa sent me to see if you needed help with supper."

"I just put the carrots and potatoes in with the roast. I need to put the bread on, but that'll be a while yet, so you are not needed at the moment."

"Is there butter for the bread?" Emily asked.

Trudie nodded. "Of course. I put some cream in a bucket under the wagon this morning, so there is some nice, fresh butter."

"Can I do something my mama taught me to do with butter? I don't have to use all of it."

"Of course." Trudie walked to the wagon and took the ball of butter she'd tucked into the back out. "How much do you need?"

"Just a small portion. I need a cup." Emily looked excited at whatever she was doing, and it thrilled Trudie to see how happy she seemed. Usually, she had a sad look when she talked about her mama.

"Anything else?" Trudie asked.

"I need honey and a fork, please."

Trudie didn't ask any more questions as she handed the girl the cup. When she poured a portion of the honey into a small amount of the butter and then stirred it diligently with the fork, Trudie grinned. Honey butter. It was something her mother had made for her when she was sick to her stomach as a child. She'd put it on toast, and Trudie's stomach would always feel better.

When Emily was finished, she held up the cup. "Honey butter! Mama wasn't the best cook, but she made the best honey butter in the whole wide world!"

"I can't wait to try it!" Trudie didn't tell Emily how much she knew she enjoyed it because she didn't want the girl to be disappointed.

"It will be the best thing you ever tasted!" Emily gave Trudie the cup. "Now I'm going back to play with my friends until supper time."

Before Trudie could say another word, the girl was off, running toward Mrs. Prewitt's wagon. Trudie followed the child, wanting to speak with Mrs. Prewitt about a bath in the morning. It had been too long since she'd soaked in a tub of hot water, rather than just using a bowl and cloth.

When Trudie reached the other woman's wagon, which was across the circle from her, she smiled in greeting. "I'd like to have a bath in the morning if you don't mind."

Mrs. Prewitt smiled and nodded. "Consider it my wedding gift."

"Oh, you don't have to do that!"

"If I don't do that, I'll have to come up with something else," Margaret said, smiling. "It's what I give all the new brides. There have been a surprising number of weddings on the trail. I guess we need to celebrate anything we can."

Trudie nodded. "That's very true. It's a hard life. Thank you for the bath, Mrs. Prewitt. I appreciate it."

"Oh, please, call me Margaret. I'll be helping with your wagon after church tomorrow."

"Then you must call me Trudie. Thank you for being willing to help. I truly appreciate it more than I can express."

"I needed help when I consolidated mine with Jamie's. There are so many things you don't need two of. We'll be leaving another wagon by the side of the trail, I guess."

Trudie nodded. "It's always strange to see an empty wagon just sitting there when we go past, but what else is to be done? It doesn't make sense to have to drive two wagons per family, unless it's a large family like the Mitchells. They *need* two wagons."

"Oh, yes, they do!" Margaret said, shaking her head. "I really admire Mrs. Mitchell, being able to take care of all those children on the trail the way she does."

"I do as well. I'm afraid I'd go mad pretty quickly, but I look forward to having Emily's companionship as we walk. She's a special girl."

Margaret smiled. "She is. She and my daughters have become fast friends, and I'm glad of it. It's so nice for them to have friends walking with them every day. It's a hard enough journey with friends. I cannot imagine it without."

Trudie contemplated the other woman's words as she walked back to her fire. She was right, of course. It was much too difficult without friends, which meant Trudie had to let her guard down, if only a little.

And not just with Joseph. With everyone in the camp. It wouldn't be easy, but she was going to have to learn to do it and still hide her history. It was possible. Somehow.

As soon as the roast was done, she took the roast, carrots, and potatoes out of the pot and used what was left to whip up some gravy. The bread was almost finished, and she looked forward to Emily's honey butter.

When she took the bread off the fire, she looked up and she saw Joseph walking toward camp with little Emily at his side. She knew they must watch her cook because they always knew exactly when to head over. Of course, after tonight, they'd be sharing a camp and it would be easy for them to know when it was time to eat.

Joseph's eyes lit up at the meat. "Where did you get a roast?" he asked.

"Mary killed a buffalo today. Penelope heard we were getting married, and she thought a roast would be nice for us to have for a wedding supper, so she brought it to me after we stopped for the day." Trudie smiled. "And Margaret is insisting I have a bath for free in the morning. I've not had a bath since I left...well, since I left for the trail."

Emily jumped up and down clapping. "It's not beans!"

Trudie laughed. "I'm so glad you're easy to please."

They all sat down, and Joseph prayed, his prayer a little more elaborate than usual. He prayed for them to have a good evening at the dance and a prosperous marriage. Trudie wasn't sure what he meant by prosperous in that connotation, but she parroted his amen at the end of the prayer anyway.

As soon as they'd eaten—the honey butter was delicious—Trudie jumped to her feet and Emily followed. "We'll do the dishes quickly tonight!" Emily announced. "I can't wait to see you married!"

Trudie smiled. "We'll be married soon enough."

Joseph stood. "I'm going to go put on my Sunday best."

"I'm just going to wear my day dress if you don't mind," Trudie said softly. It didn't make sense to her to drag out a nice dress when she was just going to change back into this one soon.

"Would you mind if I did the same?" he asked.

"Not at all."

"I'm wearing my butterfly dress Penelope made me," Emily announced to no one in particular. She was already wearing it, so it didn't need to be announced, but she obviously disagreed.

"That sounds wonderful," Trudie said. "You look so pretty in your butterfly dress."

"It magically turns me into an enchanted princess."

"It does?"

Emily nodded. "My mama always said I was her little princess, and the dress feels enchanted, so it must be."

Trudie laughed. "I think she believes in fairy tales."

"Who wouldn't?" Joseph asked, for once his eyes not looking overwhelmingly sad. Instead, they seemed to be filled with amusement.

"You have a good point, kind sir." Trudie curtseyed to him before returning to washing the dishes.

Emily giggled. "Will you teach me to curtsey just the way you do?"

"I would be honored," Trudie said grinning.

After the dishes had been stowed away, Joseph offered his arm to Trudie. "Let's go and get married."

"I'm coming!" Emily said, hurrying along beside them.

Others in the camp noticed them walking toward the preacher, and before Trudie knew what was happening, they all converged on the tent of the holy man. She hadn't expected others to be there, other than Emily of course. It was strange, but it made her feel that people of the camp could forgive her orneriness.

When the pastor announced they were man and wife and told Joseph to kiss the bride, Trudie wasn't sure what she was supposed to do. She stood for a moment, feeling as if the world was spinning around her, but then Joseph dipped his head and brushed his lips quickly against hers.

Trudie wasn't sure if she should sigh with relief that it was over or ask him to kiss her again. She hadn't expected to feel anything special when he kissed her. They had no feelings for one another after all. But the feel of his lips on hers had triggered flutters in her belly. It was surprising and completely unexpected.

Everyone stood smiling at them as they walked away from the preacher, and then someone said, "Now we dance!"

Everyone cheered, and they headed to the area where previous wagon trains had obviously held meetings and possibly church services. Trudie knew their church service would most certainly be there the following day. It was the only place where benches had been built in the area. It was always surprising to see what other companies did before them. They hadn't had to construct benches for church even once. No, the trail was fair littered with places to stay.

Joseph looked at her. "Are we headed to the dance?" he asked.

"You did promise to dance with Emily," Trudie said. "She would be very disappointed if you went back on your word."

"Then I guess we're going to the dance."

"And I will dance like a butterfly enchanted princess." Emily looked pleased with herself.

"Of course, you will. Because that's exactly what you are," Trudie said.

Emily stopped walking. "Now that you're married to Papa, I can't keep calling you Miss Brown. What should I call you?"

Trudie frowned. "Just call me Trudie. If you ever feel that you would like to call me mother or mama, you are welcome to, but for now, Trudie is fine."

Emily nodded. "That sounds good, Trudie."

Once they reached the benches where others had already taken up residence for the evening, Emily found a place for the three of them.

"You're not going to go play with your friends?" Trudie asked. Emily was a social butterfly, always with the other children.

Emily shook her head adamantly. "No. We're a family now, so we'll sit together."

"I see." Trudie looked over at Joseph, and he seemed pleased that Emily was so happy, but there was something else on his face as well.

When Emily hurried to the dance floor to spin in circles a bit later, Trudie looked over at Joseph. "Is something wrong?"

"Not really. It just seems odd that Emily is so ready to have a new mother. I thought children who'd lost a parent were more inclined to not like it when their parent married."

"I think that's usually the case," Trudie said softly, remembering how she had never wanted her mother to marry. "But Emily is a very special child. Perhaps she doesn't feel the need to mourn her mother for as long. I will tell you, though, Emily talks about your late wife constantly, so you mustn't worry that she doesn't miss her."

Joseph nodded, turning back to the dancing. "I'm glad to hear it."

Chapter Four

Saturday, June 13th, 1852

I am now a married woman. I'm not sure that my husband is very fond of me, but I know his daughter is. It seems that many of the things that I do anger him, but that's all right. I'll learn to maneuver around topics that are difficult for him, and we will get along fine.

Tomorrow I must complete the onerous task of deciding which things to take with me, and which things to leave along the side of the trail. I think someone could come without any of the supplies they want or need and still make it because of how much is left behind by others. As we drove today, I saw a beautiful rocking chair just sitting there, and I thought about getting it, but there is no space for something so frivolous. After I open my boarding house, I do believe I'll just buy another. Or if Joseph and I are still friendly, perhaps he'd make one for me.

I pray that our marriage will work out for us, and neither of us will be filled with remorse that we didn't wait longer. I do think we've done the best thing for little Emily, and that means a lot to me.

Emily danced a few dances alone, and one with the odd girl who just spun in circles around her. Trudie looked at Joseph. "How do you feel about Emily spending time with Edna Blue?"

Joseph shrugged. "Edna would never *hurt* Emily. She's just a little strange."

"More than a little," Trudie said. "She offered me a lick of the peppermint stick she carries in her cleavage, and when I said no, she stuck it in her own mouth. I can't imagine why she would keep it there." The very idea made Trudie's stomach turn. Edna was very odd.

"Her mother seems to be ill," Joseph said. "I do hope we won't lose her. We've seen how Edna is with a mother. Imagine her without one. Mrs. Blue needs to survive if only to keep being a good and calming influence on Edna."

Trudie sighed. "I've heard several of the women on the trail refer to our journey as a death march. I fear they're right."

"I won't discuss my wife's death with you!" Joseph jumped to his feet. "How dare you try to talk to me about it when you promised you wouldn't!" He looked furious, and his voice was loud enough she could feel others' eyes on them.

"That's not what I meant at all." Trudie watched helplessly as Joseph stalked toward his wagon. She didn't know what she'd done, but whatever it was, she'd be careful not to do it again. Perhaps Emily would understand.

When Emily sat down beside Trudie, she asked, "Where's Papa? He was supposed to dance with me."

"I said something that made him angry, and he walked away."

Emily frowned. "Did you mention Mama?"

"No, I promised him I never would." But his wife had been mentioned as well as her death. Perhaps Emily was onto something.

"I don't know then." Emily sighed dramatically. "He misses Mama something fierce."

"I can understand that." Trudie simply wished she knew what she'd done, so she could avoid doing it again. "Should I go talk to him?"

Emily shook her head. "No, that will just make him angrier. He'll walk for a while, and then he'll tell you he's sorry." The girl sounded wise, as if she had the entire weight of the world on her shoulders at that moment.

"Does he do this a lot?"

"Only since Mama died."

Trudie watched the dancing and listened to the music for another hour before going back to her campfire. She had a feeling she would be sleeping alone at her fire that night, and they would combine the next day. Instead, she found Joseph erecting a tent behind her wagon. "I couldn't find your tent," he said.

She shrugged. "I've been sleeping under my wagon. I didn't see a need for a tent." She wondered if he'd say something about what had happened, but he seemed to prefer to pretend nothing had.

"Well, you'll sleep in mine with Emily now, and I'll sleep under the wagon."

"I couldn't ask you to do that!" she protested. It didn't seem right for him to be the one outside when she'd not bothered to purchase what she'd need for a tent.

"Why not?" he asked. "It makes more sense than me sleeping in the tent and you under the wagon."

"All right," she said softly. "If you'll make sure your laundry is ready in the morning, I'll get it done before church. I've volunteered to sit with Mr. Bedwell to give Mrs. Gabriel a break from tending him so she could attend church. And after the service, several of the women are going to help me empty out my wagon and decide what to keep and what to leave here."

He nodded. "All right. Do you have plans for supper?" he asked.

"I'm going to make a stew out of our supper tonight. It will be filling and taste good. We should make the most out of the fresh meat while we have it."

He frowned. "Where's Emily?"

"She asked if she could stay to play with her friends a little longer, and Margaret Prewitt promised to keep an eye on her. I thought it would be good if I had a few minutes alone."

"I see. I didn't mean to yell at you earlier. I hope you'll accept my apology."

Trudie hadn't heard an apology, but she nodded anyway . "Of course. I didn't mean to say anything I shouldn't have said."

"I know."

After that, she took her bedroll out of the wagon and put it into the tent. She assumed the one already there was Emily's.

When Emily came to camp a few minutes later, her father was off fetching his own bedroll. "I'm going to sleep with you in the tent, and your papa is going to sleep under the wagon," Trudie said, forcing a smile.

"I told you everything would be good after he walked for a little while." Emily smiled. "Are you going to tell me a bedtime story?"

Trudie nodded. "I'll think of a good one if I can."

"I *know* you can."

Trudie helped Emily into her nightgown, and then the two of them lay down in the tent. Trudie hadn't bothered with a nightgown, because it was easier for her to sleep in one of her dresses. She didn't like having to leave camp in just a nightgown to take care of necessities.

As the two of them lay there talking, Trudie tried to come up with a good story to tell, and then she remembered a story her mother had told her as a child. The story had been all about Trudie and it talked of adventures she could go on.

"Once upon a time, there was a little girl named Emily," Trudie began. "The girl was brave and true, but sadly, she'd lost the person in the world most important to her. Her mama." The story went from there, telling of the girl's great bravery as she walked all the way from Missouri to Oregon.

Trudie wasn't quite finished with the adventure when Joseph crawled into the tent with them. "I came to hear your prayers, Emily."

Emily immediately knelt on the ground and put her hands together, praying for them to be a happy family and to all reach Oregon safely. When she was finished, Joseph kissed her cheek and helped her lie down, pulling her covers up to her chin. "Goodnight, Emily. I love you."

"Goodnight, Papa."

Joseph looked at his new wife. "Goodnight, Trudie. I hope you sleep well."

"Goodnight, Joseph." Trudie waited until he was gone. "Perhaps I should finish my story tomorrow."

"Oh, no, you mustn't! I need to hear if Emily catches the magical butterfly!"

Trudie laughed. "All right, but then you must sleep."

Emily sighed. "Yes, Trudie."

After the story was finished, Trudie did what her mother had always done before she fell asleep, and she dropped a kiss on the girl's forehead. "I love you, Emily. I hope your dreams are filled with all good things and are as sweet as you."

"Goodnight, Trudie. If I can't have my real mama, then I'm so glad I have you."

Outside the tent and under the wagon, Joseph heard his daughter's words. He dashed a tear from his eye. Even though he'd deprived the girl of her first mother, he'd given her a mother she could love. It may not have been what he wanted, but he knew it was the right thing for Emily.

TRUDIE WAITED UNTIL she'd finished her new family's laundry before going to Margaret for her bath. Shielded from view by the blankets Margaret had hung between the wagons, Trudie sank into the water, feeling as if she was in the most wonderful place on earth. She didn't care she was in the middle of a prairie, married to a man who had anger problems, or hiding from the police. In that moment, she was content.

After her bath, Trudie fixed a noon meal for her family, and washed her dishes. She loved to cook, but she would rather never have to wash another pot for as long as she lived. Perhaps if she ever opened the boarding house Joseph had suggested, she could hire someone to deal with the dishes, and she would do everything else for her guests.

She laughed at her thoughts as she walked toward the wagon where she would spend the next hour with Mr. Bedwell.

When she arrived, she heard Mr. Bedwell's voice raised in anger. "Why are you leaving me? You said you'd stay by my side until I was better."

Mrs. Gabriel's voice was calm as she responded. "I'm leaving to spend an hour with my family worshipping God. If you're half the man I think you are, then you will not complain or give Mrs. Simmons a hard time while she's here. She's graciously agreed to take care of you, and frankly, with your horrible temper, I need the break."

Trudie's hand covered her mouth to hide a snicker. Never had she expected someone as soft spoken and kind as Mrs. Gabriel seemed to be to talk back to Mr. Bedwell, a man who cowed all the women in camp and many of the men.

"I'm here to let you go to the church service," Trudie said with a smile. "Hello, Mr. Bedwell. Have you eaten, or can I help you?"

"I have a bowl of chicken broth here for him. Mrs. Cauldron kindly butchered one of her pullets for him to be able to have some, so he will eat it for you without complaining."

The former captain had been moved outside where he could breathe in the fresh air. He'd spent most of his time in the back of the wagon since his accident, and others had graciously packed the supplies that he was taking the place of and would return them when he was well enough to walk or drive.

Mr. Bedwell glared at Mrs. Gabriel. "I suppose I should be grateful you're not leaving me here alone to rot."

"Aye, you should. You'll not complain again of me leaving." Mrs. Gabriel put her bonnet on. "I'm looking forward to an hour of worship. If you need anything at all, don't hesitate to wait until I'm back." With that the other woman walked away, joining her children who were waiting a couple of wagons down. His children were with hers, and she smiled, and they went along with her.

Trudie didn't particularly like Mr. Bedwell, but she thought more and more of Mrs. Gabriel by the minute. "So, let's get some of this soup in you," Trudie said, sitting beside the captain on the ground.

"I don't want to eat soup. I want Katie to come back." He sounded like a petulant child to Trudie.

"Is that so? Well, you'll get her in an hour or so. Open up and I'll feed you your soup." Trudie never would have spoken that way to the man until she heard Mrs. Gabriel stand up to him. Now he seemed...well, not quite so scary in her eyes.

It was a long hour, but every time the man opened his mouth to complain, Trudie shoved another spoonful of soup into his mouth. It worked well, because she didn't have to listen to him, and he received the nutrition he was obviously needing.

When the bowl was empty, she wondered for a moment what to do, but then she heard voices of everyone coming back into camp after their service. "He ate the whole bowl," Trudie said as Mrs. Gabriel came back to the wagon.

"Better than I expected," Mrs. Gabriel said with a smile. "Thank you so much for giving me some time with my children. They're afraid to come too close to him because he's so surly."

"Then I'm doubly glad I thought to ease your burden a little. If he's still sick next week, I'll sit with him again."

Mr. Bedwell protested. "No, you won't! You wouldn't let me speak and kept shoving broth in my mouth every time I tried."

"I'd do it again, too," Trudie said, winking at Mrs. Gabriel. "I'm going to go talk to the pastor now and suggest that you are nominated for sainthood."

Mrs. Gabriel laughed. "I like you, Mrs. Simmons."

"And I like you! You let me know if you need another break and have a bowl of broth at the ready, and I'm happy to help."

"Sounds like a good plan to me." Mrs. Gabriel sat down beside Mr. Bedwell. "Are you still hungry?"

Trudie walked back toward her wagon instead of staying to listen to the conversation between caretaker and patient. When she got back to her campsite, there were eight women standing there ready to help her. Penelope, who was the only person on the trail she felt she could call friend, smiled at her. "Let's get this going!"

The women all joked and laughed as they worked together. "The best part of being on this God-forsaken trail is the women we get to spend time with. You're all my sisters. Well, except for you, Mary. You're my daughter." Mrs. Mitchell grinned at her daughter.

Trudie was quiet as she listened to the others, not having much to contribute other than a nod or a headshake when someone held something up for her to make a decision on. They moved all the food from her wagon into Joseph's, and she knew they were close to halfway. They had more provisions than they should at this point of the journey, and she was pleased.

"I still want to get a kill this afternoon," Mary said to no one in particular. "Will I have help drying the meat if do?"

For the first time, Trudie felt like she had something to contribute. "I'd love to help."

Mary smiled at her. "Good. Everyone who helps gets a share of the meat, both the fresh and the dry."

"That would be wonderful," Trudie said, knowing she could feed her family for much longer if they had more meat in their diet. It was hard to make the provisions stretch, and she knew they'd be getting putrid before too long.

Betty walked over to stand next to Trudie. "You seem different."

Trudie nodded. "I'm trying hard. I'm sorry I was so rude to you. I simply don't like to talk about what was before the trail. This has to be my life from now on."

"I understand," Betty said softly. "I truly do. And I'm happy you are making some friends among the other women."

Wondering if that was true, Trudie got back to work. She didn't know if she was making real friends, the kind who would stand by her through anything. But she was making plenty of friendly acquaintances, and that pleased her a great deal.

When the task was finished, Mary said, "I'm going to go get Bob, and we're going to get some game."

"Sounds wonderful," Hannah—the pastor's wife—told Mary. Trudie envied the friendship between the other two women. They'd somehow become fast friends before they'd even left Independence.

After everyone was gone, Trudie started the stew she planned for supper. She wanted to be able to do as much as she could to help with the meat.

Joseph walked to her as soon as he saw her at their campfire. "Everything done?"

She nodded. "Yes, with all those hands helping, the work was easy."

"Good. I'm on watch for the next few hours, so I'll want you to look after Emily."

"Yes, of course. If I hadn't had so much that needed to be done today, I'd have been watching her all day."

"That's your job as a wife," Joseph said, walking away.

"Emily and I will bring you stew when it's ready," she called after him.

"No need. Just save me a bit, and I'll eat it when I come back to camp."

Trudie's first instinct was to ignore him and take the food to him anyway, but she didn't want to face his anger again. She didn't know what would set the man off, and she had no desire to find out.

Emily stood watching Trudie cook for a moment. "Is there anything I can do to help?"

Trudie shook her head. "No, but why don't you invite Sally and Amanda to come and play with you here, and I'll watch you both so their mother can have a break."

"Do mothers need breaks from being mothers?" the child asked, looking genuinely confused.

"You know, I think some do. You have to worry about your child all the time. Are they too close to the river? Are they stepping on a snake? Are they happy? Having some time to just be Margaret and not be mama for a while will make Margaret a *better* mother."

Emily seemed to consider Trudie's words for a moment, and then she nodded. "All right. I'll go ask them to play." And Emily ran off toward the other children. Soon the three of them were back, and then Betty's daughter, Annie, joined them. It was fun to watch them play.

It was such a simple little thing they did. Playacting that they were on a farm in Oregon Territory, and they were watching for Indians. Well, one was watching for Indians. One was making tea and serving pretend cookies on leaves. All the others called her "Mama." The other two sat and played with pretend dolls and acted as if they were much younger than they really were.

It was endearing, and it told Trudie something she'd known long ago, but had forgotten in recent months. She wanted children of her own. But she was married to a man who had no feelings for her. Perhaps it was time she opened up to him a little so they could build trust between them. She wasn't sure if it would work, but she did want to be able to have a real life.

Of course, she wasn't certain if she'd stay with Joseph and Emily, but every day with the little girl made her love her even more. Soon, she wouldn't be able to leave even if she wanted to.

Trudie sighed. It was a dilemma, but it wasn't one that had to be solved immediately. No, that decision could wait for another day.

Chapter Five

Monday, June 15th, 1852

We finally made it to Independence Rock today, and it was such an incredible experience to carve my name onto a rock that many others have carved their names into and many more will for years to come. It made me feel both mighty and insignificant at the same time. Mighty, because I am now a part of history and people will talk about the Oregon Trail for years to come. But insignificant because my name is just one of many on that rock.

Independence Rock means that we are halfway to Oregon City. Halfway to claiming the land that will forge our futures. Some days I think we all lose sight of what we are migrating across this great land for, and then there are days like today, where we are all reminded why we are going to Oregon. For free land. For new opportunities. Today was a day of celebration, and all of our moods were lighter after spending our noon break near the rock that means so much to so many people.

What a joyous experience, carving my name on a rock. I hope people will always have something as significant in their lives—something to work and strive for. Something to make them believe they are truly making a difference in this world—one step at a time.

Her first day of walking with the other women, Trudie found enlightening. She hadn't imagined the camaraderie that would happen during the long walk, instead she'd imagined that the women were just as solitary as the men as they drove the wagons.

Instead, she was part of much laughter and talking as they moved. She walked with Penelope, Hannah, Mary, Betty, Mrs. Cauldron, and Margaret. The other women spoke of what they wanted to do once they reached Oregon, and they talked about the area where they planned to live. Mrs. Cauldron looked sad when they brought it up, and Trudie asked her why.

"My husband and I are traveling west to live near some very dear friends of ours. I am looking forward to seeing those friends and living near them, but it's so hard to say goodbye to those I've grown to love on the trail." Mrs. Cauldron shook her head. "I know it will be good for the twins to start with a fresh reputation because everyone considers them trouble makers, but I'm sad for me."

Trudie nodded. "I do understand." She'd felt the same when she'd moved from the household where she'd grown up as her mother's assistant to a household where she was the main cook. Leaving all the people she'd known and loved behind for a new position had been very difficult, but her mother had encouraged her to do just that. It wasn't long after she'd moved on that her mother had been run down by a carriage that had been unable to stop.

Betty looked at her sister, Mrs. Cauldron. "I do wish you were settling near the rest of us. I need my sister."

"We'll be able to write letters, but it won't be the same." Mrs. Cauldron sighed. "My children will grow up without knowing their cousins or how very much you adore them."

"I know Wyoming Territory is vast, but surely we'll be able to visit some. At least I hope we will. I can't imagine not living near you."

Trudie felt her heart going out to the sisters. She'd never had a sister herself, but she'd always known that if she had, they'd have been close friends. Of course, that would have meant leaving a loved one behind when she'd had to run. No, it was better that she had no family left back east.

They stopped at Independence Rock for their noon meal, and each of the travelers carved their name into the rock. Trudie had to wonder if the names would still be legible long into the future or if they'd be washed away with time. Either way, it felt like a rite of passage to carve their names into the rock. And more importantly, it meant they were halfway to Oregon City and getting a parcel of free land. She didn't yet know if she'd be sharing a larger parcel with Joseph and Emily or finding one of her own, but either way, life would be different once they were off the trail. Life on the trail was difficult, but now that she was getting to know people, Trudie knew she'd miss the life she had while traveling.

As they finished the noon meal, the captains gathered everyone together. Mr. Cauldron spoke loudly enough for everyone to hear. "We are at the halfway point between Independence and Oregon City, and we are almost a month ahead of where we need to be. We thought we'd leave it to everyone to take a vote to decide if we should spend the rest of the day at this important spot and move on tomorrow or if we want to move on after our mid-day rest."

Trudie was surprised. The company had never voted on something so important as to whether to move on or not, but she was well aware that only the men's opinions mattered, so she waited to see what would happen.

The men's votes were cast with "ayes" and "nays." The "nays" won, and they decided to keep going. They didn't want to lose the advantage that being one of the first wagons of the season to arrive in Oregon would give them.

Trudie wasn't sure if she was happy or disappointed that they were moving on, but she knew it didn't matter either way. She must do what the others wanted and continue to move on. Further from New York and the scene of her crime was always good.

Putting Emily into the back of the wagon to nap, Trudie joined the other women and they began their afternoon's trek. Mary was the most vocal of the bunch. "I for one think the men made the right decision. The sooner we get to Oregon, the sooner we can start our new lives."

Hannah nodded in agreement. "It was the best decision, especially after we laid over for so long last week with the difficult crossing of the river. I do hope we can reach our final destination—wherever it may be—before the snows fall."

"Good point," Margaret said. "I wouldn't enjoy traveling with little ones through the snow. It's hard enough as it is. And it's going to be harder soon." She placed her hand on her belly. "I'm pretty sure I'm expecting my third."

There were many smiles of delight, and only Mrs. Mitchell seemed alarmed. "This journey is hard enough for women who are not with child. I will pray for you."

"Thank you," Margaret said.

Hannah linked her arm through Margaret's. "I'm just happy that you're going to have a baby so soon. I wish I could say I was expecting as well."

Mrs. Mitchell simply shook her head. "It will be better if you wait until we reach our new homes."

"I don't always tend to do what's best, Mrs. Mitchell," Hannah said with a smile.

"There are so many dangerous mountain passes we have to endure yet. I worry for any of the women who have little ones or who are expecting."

Mary sighed. "Mama, you worry enough for the whole company, and there's no worry left for the rest of us."

"Mind your tongue, Mary!"

"I will do my best, but you know I've never been good at minding my tongue. Shooting is something I'm awfully good at, but minding my tongue is something else entirely."

Her mother sighed dramatically. "I don't know where I went wrong with you."

Mary laughed. "I think you went right with me. There's not a thing wrong with being a wild woman who does as she pleases."

Mrs. Mitchell simply shook her head.

"What do you plan to do when we reach Oregon?" Penelope asked Trudie. Trudie tended to stick close to Penelope as they walked, knowing she would be mindful of asking questions.

"I was thinking of opening a café, but Joseph thinks a boarding house would be better."

"If you're settling near the rest of us, I would say go with the boarding house. I do believe Margaret is planning to open a diner."

Margaret grinned at them. "Yes, I am. But perhaps we should go into business together. We could have a boarding house with an adjoining restaurant. Then people passing through who don't want to stay with you could still eat."

A slow smile crossed Trudie's lips. "You'd be willing to go into business with me?" It had never occurred to her that anyone on their wagon train would ever want to see her again once the trip was over.

"I would! You seem like you would be a shrewd businesswoman, and I like the idea of having someone like that at my side through all of life's adventures. Hopefully we'll take turns having babies so neither of us will feel overwhelmed."

"I'm not sure there are babies in my future," Trudie said softly. She knew they weren't if her marriage with Joseph stayed the way it was.

"There's no greater reward in life than children," Margaret responded, her hand going again to her flat belly.

"And no greater responsibility," Mrs. Mitchell said. "You don't want to have a girl who grows up to be like my Mary."

Mary said nothing, but she made a face behind her mother's back causing the others to laugh.

"I think we all appreciate Mary's skills," Hannah said softly. "We certainly wouldn't be eating as well on this journey as we have without her along."

"That's very true," Margaret said, nodding emphatically. "I fill my pot with Mary's meats almost every night, and she doesn't allow me to pay for the food. I almost feel guilty charging those who eat at my fire. Almost."

"I'm doing what I love by hunting. You're cooking for some extra money in your pocket once we arrive in Oregon." Mary shrugged.

"Jamie keeps telling me to stop cooking for others, but I can't let them go hungry. And having the extra money can't hurt."

"No, it can't," Mrs. Mitchell said. "Mr. Prewitt will realize soon enough that he's blessed to have a wife who is willing to work and make money for her family."

"I do hope you're right," Margaret said. "Now that we're pretty sure I'm expecting, he tells me to slow down every single day. But I can't and meet the goal I set for myself before we left Independence. When I lost my first husband, I was left destitute. I will never be in that position again."

The strength in Margaret's voice came through. She was a strong-willed woman, and Trudie was sure it was a good thing.

Trudie made a gravy with jerky that night, serving it over biscuits. She worried their flour wouldn't last much longer, and she wanted to save the potatoes she had left for later meals. Of course, the potatoes wouldn't last much longer either. She was a bit worried about what they would do when the provisions ran out, but she had to trust in God and Mary's musket.

After saying the prayer, Joseph asked Trudie, "How was your first day of walking with the other women?"

"Surprisingly good," she answered. "I didn't realize what kind of fun the women had walking and talking together. I guess I thought their experience was similar to mine, sitting alone driving."

"Oh, no," Emily said. "We have lots of fun walking. I could have told you that!"

Trudie grinned. "I'm sure you could have."

Joseph smiled at his daughter. "And how was your day walking?"

"It was ever so much fun," Emily said. "We walked and sang songs and threw rocks. And Trudie helped me write my name on the big rock. Inpence Rock."

Trudie smiled. "Independence Rock. All the settlers are carving their names into the rock."

"Why?" Emily asked.

"So, the people who come through here in ten years will know we were here," Joseph answered. "It's a long hard journey, and I think it helps people to know others have made it. And the rock means we're halfway to Oregon."

"So, our journey is half over?" Emily asked excitedly.

"No, it's not. We're halfway to Oregon City, but we will have to then choose our new land and go to that new land. It will take us a good deal more time to get where we want to go," Joseph said.

"But why?"

"Why are we going to Oregon City if that's not where we're settling?" he asked.

Emily nodded.

"Because we have to file our land claims there. We can't just go to the land we want and call it our own."

"Oh. Why not?" Emily asked.

Trudie hid a smile at the girl's questions. She'd wondered the same thing before the journey.

"Because if we go to the land, and someone else claims it, it becomes their land and not ours. We want to get our land legally so we can live there forever, and not have someone else be able to make us leave."

"But if we claim the land, they can't make us go?" Emily asked.

"That's right. And we're going to live on the land we claim forever."

"With Trudie?"

Joseph didn't seem to know how to answer that. "If Trudie wants to live with us forever, then she will stay with us."

"Oh." Emily looked at Trudie with wide eyes, as if she expected her to disappear at any moment. "You won't leave us, will you?"

"I have no plans of leaving you." Trudie reached out and stroked the child's shoulder. "You're my daughter now." And that's when Trudie realized that no matter what happened between her and Joseph, she would never leave Emily. The girl would need to always be hers.

After the meal, Trudie and Emily washed the dishes together while Joseph went to check on the livestock. As soon as the dishes were stowed away, Emily went to play with her friends, and Trudie took some mending to Penelope's campfire, where some of the other women were gathered. She didn't really contribute to the conversation going on around her, but it was good to feel like she was included and part of the group.

As she sat there, she thought about how far she'd come since February when Mr. Whathisbutt had died. She'd run all the way to Chicago without thinking. Well, she'd *traveled* there without thinking, hoping to lose herself in the city, but she'd looked over her shoulder everywhere she'd gone. Many had been talking about traveling west, and she'd decided to change her name and join a company going west.

Making her way to Independence hadn't been easy, for people were mistrustful of women traveling alone, but once she'd met up with a group traveling to Oregon, she'd tried to blend into the background. It had mostly worked until she and Penelope had become friends.

Now, it was a matter of making it to Oregon City and deciding where to live with her new family. Anyone looking for her would be looking for someone with a different name, traveling alone. But now she was married and had changed her name twice. She prayed nightly that she was safe and wouldn't endanger her new family or the others in the company.

When Mrs. Gabriel joined the group around the fire, Trudie smiled at her. "How did you get away?"

Mrs. Gabriel shook her head. "I gave him a little of the laudanum the doctor gave me for his lungs. Just a touch, but it was enough to knock him out. He was in pain, but to be truthful, I wanted him to sleep more than anything. He's very ornery today."

"Why?" Trudie asked. And if Mrs. Gabriel was saying he was ornery today, Trudie wanted to know what he'd been the previous day. She'd never been around anyone ornerier.

"He's healing, but the doctor doesn't want him driving or walking yet, so he complains about every bump along the trail. I swear if I was a drinking woman, I'd be drowning my sorrows with whatever I could find today."

Trudie laughed. "How are you going to return to him in the morning?"

"I sleep near him every night to be sure he has no needs." Mrs. Gabriel shook her head. "If he hadn't saved my daughter, I'm not sure I would be taking the time to care for him."

"Yes, you would," Trudie said softly. "I saw you with him. You should be a nurse. You're so good at dealing with sick people." Trudie had thought she was skilled in caring for others until she'd seen Mrs. Gabriel with their cantankerous former captain.

"I have no time to be anyone's nurse. I have children to care for, who are starting to feel neglected."

"Should I invite them to eat with my family?" Trudie asked.

Mrs. Gabriel shook her head. "I cook for them. They just eat a couple of wagons down from us, so they don't have to be the object of Mr. Bedwell's temper."

"I hope he gets less angry as he gets better."

"I do believe he will. He's a good man, deep down. So deep none of the rest of us can see it, but it's there. Somewhere."

Trudie hid a smile. "I suppose he must be if you're still taking care of him every day."

When she climbed into the tent with Emily a short while later, Trudie continued the adventures of Emily, telling the girl about the incredible journey they were on, but making it a magical journey, filled with fairies and leprechauns, just as her mother had done for her as a girl.

Joseph stood outside the tent for a long while, listening to the yarn Trudie was spinning about Emily and her adventures. He couldn't help but smile as she made it seem like the trail was a tremendous adventure meant for children. He knew his first wife had only seen it as a back-breaking journey, and she'd begged him every day for more than a year not to make her go. When he had, she'd been sad and dejected. Of course, his wife had always been sad and dejected.

He'd done the right thing for him, but by doing so, he'd deprived his daughter of a mother, and he'd killed his wife. He hated to admit that he hadn't done everything he should do to care for the woman he'd promised to cherish all of his life. Surely, he should have done better.

He stood like that for half an hour listening before reminding himself that he had to be up before sunrise to be on the trail as quickly as possible. He listened to his daughter pray and tucked her in, saying goodnight to both Emily and Trudie. As he crawled under the wagon, he couldn't help but think about what a good mother Trudie was for Emily.

Perhaps things needed to change between him and his new wife...in time. He wanted to take things slowly, much slower than he had with Emily's mother. He'd met her and three days later, she'd been his wife—after much cajoling on his part. They'd been terribly mismatched as husband and wife. She'd been a timid woman who preferred not to leave her home often, and he'd longed for adventure. He'd wanted to give her the world and thought the only way he could do so was going west. And she would have been happy living with her parents for the rest of her life. No, they hadn't been a good match, but that didn't mean he hadn't loved her with everything inside him.

Chapter Six

Saturday, June 20th, 1852

Walking is much harder work than I'd imagined it would be. The women walk all day long, and then have to cook supper and clean up after it. The men find this journey an adventure, but for the women, it's just working harder than ever before. I look forward to opening a business because it will feel like a rest after the work of the trail.

I told Joseph the truth about my past at the dance tonight, and he told me what he's been hiding as well. I feel as if my story is so much worse than his, and I wait to find out if he can accept me for who I am, or if he wants me to part from him and Emily when we reach Oregon City.

We talked about the possibility of a real courtship and marriage tonight, which is why I felt the need to tell him the truth about what I did. I'm not sure it's something he'll be able to forgive, but we've agreed to have a long walk and discuss it tomorrow. I do hope things can work out between us. I cannot imagine my life without little Emily. She brings joy to everyone she comes into contact with.

By that Saturday, Trudie's legs were so sore, she was sure she'd never be able to walk another inch. Of course, the soreness in her arms was finally getting better. Driving the oxen was just as difficult as walking all day.

They were now far from the river they'd followed for so long, and it felt as if they were in a different land entirely. The nights were quite cool, and the days were hot, but it was a dry heat. Trudie had to keep reminding herself that every step she took was one step closer to Oregon.

At the dance, she was careful to say little to Joseph except about Emily. Talking about his daughter always seemed to keep him in a good mood instead of a foul one.

Emily dragged him out onto the "dance floor" twice. When Joseph returned to Trudie the second time, he held his hand out to her. "May I have this dance?"

Trudie's heart fluttered, feeling as if she was being courted for the first time in her life. She'd never attended a dance before their journey, other than attending as a maid taking care of food and drinks. Now she was actually going to dance for the first time in her life. "I've never danced before," she said softly.

He smiled. "I have. Just follow my lead." With her hand in his, he led her to where the other dancers were, carefully side-stepping Bob and Mary who made quite a spectacle of themselves.

When Joseph took her into his arms, Trudie felt shivers all over her body. Being held by him—by any man—felt strange. It was certainly different than being touched by Mr. Baldwin She reveled in the feel of Joseph's arms around her, and she had no desire to push him away. When he pulled her closer to avoid being trampled by Edna Blue, she expected him to immediately release her, but he never did. Instead, he held her close until the dance was over, and then he walked back to where they'd been sitting together.

"That was really nice," Trudie said softly. "Thank you for asking me to dance with you." She'd been surprised, but it had been a good thing. Perhaps having a man's arms around her wasn't as horrible as she'd thought.

He smiled at her. "I enjoyed it as well. We'll have to do it more often."

"I'd like that." She wanted to ask him if he'd danced with Emily's mother often, but she had to obey their strict "no questions" policy.

"I want to thank you for the stories you tell Emily at night. I've never heard anything like them." He sat down beside her, giving her his full attention, which never seemed to happen.

She smiled. "My mother always told me adventures about Gertrude. I thought Emily would enjoy it if I made her the heroine of her bedtime stories."

"Gertrude?" he asked. "Is that your full name?"

Trudie's eyes widened. "It is, but I'd prefer you not use it." She looked around as if someone would have heard her first name—a name held by thousands of other women—and know she was a murderess.

His eyes seemed full of understanding. "I will never use it again."

"Thank you," she said softly.

"But I do like *knowing* your real name." He wanted to know everything about her now, and he hated that he'd made that silly agreement with her to never ask her questions about his past. He felt more drawn to her every day, though he was fighting the feelings. How could he have forgotten about his first wife for long enough to even find another woman attractive? She hadn't been dead for a full two months yet.

"Just make sure to think of me as Trudie so my real name isn't used. Trudie is what me mam called me when I was a girl, and I prefer to be called by it now. It reminds me of her." And it was a different name than anyone back east would remember her by.

"Is she still alive?" Joseph asked, hoping the question wouldn't feel too intrusive to her.

Trudie considered for a moment before responding. "She's not. She died a few years back. She was run over by a carriage when she was trying to cross the street. She was knocked down and one of the horses stomped on her head."

"I'm so sorry for your loss."

Trudie nodded. "Thank you. It's been a long time, but I still miss her every day." She shook her head. "And your parents? Do they live?"

"They do. They are still in Virginia, wishing I didn't have wandering feet."

"And you can't blame them for that. You took their granddaughter from them."

"I did. My mother begged me not to come." The subject was getting too close to his late wife for his comfort, so he immediately switched topics. "Have you thought more about whether you want to have a café or a boarding house?"

"The more I think about it, the more the boarding house idea is growing on me. Margaret Prewitt plans to open a diner wherever the company settles and asked me if I'd like to do a combination boarding house and diner. We would manage them together."

"I like that idea actually. Were you planning on settling near the rest?"

"Not until she suggested that. I hadn't thought about it before that really," she lied. She'd thought about it a lot, but since she knew she'd be changing her name, she hadn't truly considered *doing* it.

"If you'd like to settle with the others in the company, I would be open to that. I just need some open land to ranch."

"I think...well, I think I would like that if you would. We know everyone and feel safe with them. How would you feel?"

He shrugged. "I'd like that you and Emily would have friends, and we'd be near a doctor. Truly it seems like a good idea to me."

"Then we should do just that. I like the idea of having friends there already. I'm sure everyone is looking for the right place as we go along. I believe we're already in Oregon Territory, and now we just need to find the right place to settle."

"What kind of place sounds good to you?" he asked.

"I want to be away from cities, of course. Growing up in a city, it's always been my dream to live in the country, surrounded by trees and mountains. Maybe having a creek or a lake nearby, but I don't want to live on the lake. I want any children to be safe."

"Children?" he asked. "Are you thinking about having more children?"

She shrugged. "I wouldn't be disappointed if it happened. I've always loved children, and Emily has reminded me how very much I want some of my own." She felt daring mentioning it to him, but it was the truth.

"Do you want to have a real marriage with me then?" Joseph wasn't sure how he felt about the idea, but he couldn't deny his attraction to her.

"I don't think either of us are quite ready for that." She couldn't imagine being held down the way Mr. Baldwin had held her down. No, she definitely wasn't ready for a real marriage yet. Someday, but not today.

"How would you feel if I courted you then? I know we'd be doing everything backward, but I'd love to take you for walks in the evening and sit with you and get to know you better."

Trudie bit her lip thinking about it. "But you won't do anything to me without my permission, right? You won't...hurt me?"

His eyes widened, and he took her hand, pulling her to her feet and away from the dancing and music. "Has someone raped you, Trudie?"

She shook her head. "No, but someone tried. And I killed him."

He stared at her, shocked by her words. "And that's what you're running from?"

She nodded. "I didn't want to kill him, but I pushed him away from me, and he tumbled over a bannister. And he died. And I changed my name and ran as far as I could. So now you know the truth. You're married to a thief and a murderess."

"A thief?" Joseph was still trying to wrap his head around everything she was saying. The sweet gentle woman in front of him had killed a man? How was that even possible?

"I went into his bedroom and stole three pieces of his wife's jewelry. It paid for me to get out of the city and get everything I needed for the trip to Oregon." She combed her fingers through her hair in despair. He must hate her now. How could he not? "I didn't mean to kill him, but I *did* mean to steal the jewelry to get away. I didn't know what else to do."

"I'm not sure what I should say."

"I'm not either, but now you know everything I've been hiding. The man I killed was my employer, and he'd raped several of the maids who worked for him. One was pregnant with his child, but was sent away by his wife, who had no idea her husband was the baby's father." Trudie took a deep breath. "I would never have killed him deliberately, but I couldn't let him do that to me. He frightened me so."

"I'm sure he did. I had no idea." And he had no idea how he was supposed to react now that he knew his daughter was sleeping in a tent every night with a woman who had killed a man. "Can we talk about this again tomorrow? Perhaps we can go for a walk after church?"

She nodded. "I'm sure Margaret would be happy to keep an eye on Emily while we talked." She looked away from him, watching Edna weave in and out of the people on the dancefloor with her arms spread wide. How she avoided bumping into everyone, Trudie would never know. "I know I should have told you all this before I married you. But I'm telling you now. We can't have a real marriage with this between us."

"No, we can't. And you need to know something as well." He took a ragged breath. "I killed my wife."

TRUDIE'S DREAMS WERE worse than ever that night. But this time after she pushed Mr. Baldwin over the balcony, Joseph was there, pointing at her, and calling her a murderess. Then he was wearing a policeman's hat and when Mr. Baldwin grabbed her ankle from the floor and pulled her down with him, he held up handcuffs and laughed at her.

She woke up well before dawn, the nightmares fresh in her mind, and she got up and started a fire. There was no need to lie there in the dark, tormented by her thoughts. It was easier to be moving around and concentrating on things that must be done.

Trudie wasn't surprised when Joseph joined her at the fire she built. "I've been thinking about everything you told me last night," he said softly. "I understand what happened."

"You do?" she asked, surprised. "I thought you'd tell me you never wanted to speak to me again once we reached Oregon City."

"What about what I told you?" he asked.

"It didn't make sense. We all know your wife died of cholera." Trudie waited for him to tell her what he'd meant by his startling statement.

"I forced her to go to Oregon. She begged me not to make her go. She cried and cried, telling me she couldn't live without being close to her parents. The idea of going through Indian country frightened her so much. But I didn't listen. I had itchy feet, and I felt the need to leave everything we knew and set out on an adventure. In Virginia, I never would have been more than the son of a dirt farmer, but in the west, I can be *anything*. I wanted to give her the world, and instead, I dragged her to her death, leaving Emily without a mother."

"You can't blame yourself for her death. Half the men in this company forced their women to go west. How can you blame yourself for what happened?" Trudie couldn't believe he likened taking his wife west with her killing her former employer. The two acts were very different.

"I see my action as being much worse than yours," he said softly. "I did something terrible to someone I love. You were protecting yourself."

"So, you think you can court me and potentially have a real marriage, even though you know my past?" It was hard to believe he was willing to even try with her.

"If you can do the same with me." Joseph didn't understand why she was surprised. She hadn't deliberately killed a man. His actions were worse than hers. In his eyes anyway.

"I can. I don't think you did anything wrong."

"And I don't think you did."

She took a deep breath. "I will ask that you'll still be circumspect about what I've said. I don't want anyone to know." She didn't want to think the people she was becoming friends with would look at her differently.

"I won't tell a soul." He hid his yawn behind his hand. "Why are you up so early?"

She sighed. "I have nightmares. I still see the man I killed falling over the banister to his death. I didn't want to wake Emily, so I got up instead."

"That makes sense." He watched her mix some things together. "Spoiling her with johnny cakes again?"

"Johnny cakes, bacon, and tea. I wish she could drink coffee, but she's doing well with the tea as long as I add a good amount of honey."

"She'll eat or drink anything if it has enough honey on it." He leaned back on his hands, watching her cook. He was surprised by how pretty she was. He hadn't really looked at her the way he was now. Sure, he'd noticed that he was physically attracted to her, but he was certain that was just their proximity to one another. Knowing she was pretty...well, he wished he hadn't noticed. He might have to court her for a good long while before he could bed her.

Emily woke up excitedly when she saw the breakfast Trudie was making. "Sunday is the only day you can sleep late," Trudie told the girl. "I would think you'd take advantage of it."

Emily shook her head. "Sunday is the only day when I get to play all day long!"

Trudie hid a grin, but Joseph shook his head. "You can help Trudie with the wash today."

"The wash!" Emily frowned. "I don't like washing clothes."

"I'm sure Trudie doesn't either." Joseph gave the girl a stern look.

"Yes, Papa. But I don't have to like it."

"No, you don't." Joseph shook his head at her. "I'm going to have to get one of the oxen reshoed today, and that will take a while. And then I have watch duty during church."

"Do you know if the former captain is on his feet yet?" Trudie asked, thinking about her promise to Mrs. Gabriel to sit with him again if he wasn't healed this week.

"I saw him walking around earlier. He's supposed to be alternating riding sitting up this week with walking. I can just imagine how he'll react to walking with the women."

"I'm sure he'll be at church service then. I'll be able to go with Emily." Trudie wasn't certain if she was happy or sad about that. She still felt as if God had forsaken her with Mr. Baldwin, but she knew she needed to get back to church to slowly build her faith again. She hadn't regularly attended church since before she'd left New York.

"Good. I'll be back for lunch, but that's probably the only time you'll see me before supper. And I'd like it if you'd ask Mrs. Prewitt to watch Emily after supper this evening. I wish to take my wife for a walk."

Trudie looked down at her food, trying to keep him from seeing her blush. She wasn't used to a man courting her, and it felt strange to allow it to happen.

The morning wash went quickly with the chattering that went with it. There was only a small creek to wash clothes in, instead of the river. But it was the last time they may be able to wash clothes for weeks, so they had to take advantage. Now that they were no longer traveling along the river, water would be more scarce.

During the church service, Emily sat close to Trudie, and Trudie kept her arm around the little girl, who ended up falling asleep against Trudie. Trudie tried to listen to the sermon, but her mind was on the walk she'd take with her husband that evening. They'd been married a week but had only shared one kiss and one dance. Perhaps after their walk, it would all be different.

After spending some time talking to the other women after the service, Trudie walked back to her camp until she heard a shotgun. Someone was trying to get some meat.

When Mary came back to camp with Bob beside her, between the two of them, they carried a doe that was immediately strung up in a tree. There would be fresh meat that night, if there was enough for Trudie's family, and she hoped there would be. It was so much easier to cook tasty dishes with fresh meat than with dried. And she did her best never to get out the beans, which Emily hated so much, but they were filling and lasted longer than most of their supplies, so she didn't have a lot of choice when there was no fresh meat.

Sure enough, Mary offered to share, and Trudie was given enough meat to cook supper and have a little leftover for their noon meal the next day. Trudie thanked the other woman profusely.

Mary shook her head. "You just have to remember who fed you on the trail when I'm asking you to cook for me when we settle."

Trudie smiled and nodded. "I'd be delighted to give you a free meal from time to time, as that's what you're doing for us."

"And maybe I could be your official provider of meat for the boarding house."

"That's a wonderful idea. If you can provide fresh game, I'm sure we can get fresh beef from Joseph. He plans to be a rancher."

"Bob's still trying to decide between farming and ranching. Whichever he decides on, I'm sure he'll be happy to provide you with fresh something."

Trudie smiled. "That's the plan then." As she walked back toward her fire, she realized she was truly making friends now, and if God was good, they would be friends who would last a lifetime.

Chapter Seven

Sunday, June 21ˢᵗ, 1852

I walked with Joseph this evening, and it was lovely. He held my hand and picked flowers for me. It seems as if he can look past what I've done and still want to have a real marriage with me.

With my history, and his wife's recent death, we are moving slowly. Emily needs to have us together for a long time, and that's what we will attempt to do.

I am thankful that God put Emily and Joseph into my life because they've taught me that no matter what, I can continue on with my life. One day at a time. One step at a time. We will get where we're going when we arrive there. I'm not known for my patience, but that is just fine. Together, we will reach our destination in our own time.

Their walk after supper that night was different than the ones they'd gone on before. For one thing, Joseph held Trudie's hand as they walked. It felt a great deal more intimate to her than just walking side by side. And he stopped to pick her some flowers that grew alongside the trail. She wasn't sure if they were truly flowers or weeds, but they smelled nice and looked pretty, and that was all that really mattered.

He talked a little about his wife, Alice, and Trudie listened quietly. She wasn't about to ask questions when they'd both made it clear that questions weren't acceptable.

"She was a shy thing. I met her at the store in town one day, and when I tried to talk to her, she blushed and went over to stand beside her mother. I think she may have been too young to be ready to marry, but her parents really encouraged her to accept me as her husband. She was only sixteen, and I was nineteen at the time."

"That *is* young." At sixteen, Trudie had still been an apprentice cook under her mother. She couldn't imagine marrying so young.

"I probably should have waited, but I was ready to start my life as a married man. We had Emily right off, which probably wasn't great for her either. After the baby was born, she had no desire to ever leave the house without me. I had to take time off from working my father's land with him just to take her to the store in town for the supplies we needed." He shook his head. "When I first brought up going west, she got me to agree to wait a year. And then another year. She kept saying Emily was too small to make the trek. And then she finally admitted that she didn't want to live so far from her parents. Her mother visited with her almost every day. I think if her mother hadn't been there to talk to her, she'd have ventured out more and learned to stand on her own two feet."

"I can see that. When I started cooking for a different family than my mother did, I visited with my mother every Sunday morning. And then after she died...well, I felt like I had to be an adult and on my own. I already was, but I knew I had my mother to lean on if I ever needed to." Trudie shrugged. "It was better once I was completely on my own, though, because I took responsibility for my own actions."

"How long did you work for the family you were working for before you left for the trail?" he asked. He tried to avoid mentioning the horrible thing that had happened, but he still wanted to know the answer.

"Three years. I started working for them when I was eighteen."

"So, you're twenty-one now?"

She nodded. "I am."

"I'm twenty-five now. It's hard to believe you're younger than my first wife. You seem so much more...sure of yourself." Joseph was impressed with the woman who stood beside him. She was strong and seemed ready to face the world in a way Emily's mother had never been.

"I was a different person six months ago. Having to run from people and constantly hide makes you confident quickly. You have no choice in the matter."

"That makes a lot of sense to me. I do wish I'd courted Emily's mother for a couple of years before I actually married her. Perhaps everything would have been different then." Joseph seemed to think he'd made a big mistake.

"You know, looking back makes it easy to know what to do. I'm sure you did what you thought was best at the time."

"I did." He sighed. "And I wouldn't have Emily if I'd done things differently. I don't know what I'd do without Emily."

Trudie smiled. "She's such a special little girl. I've never known anyone like her. She's so full of life!"

"That's a good way to put it," Joseph said with a smile. "She spent so much time in our tiny little house with her mother back east that she's excited to be outside, doing what she wants to do and having other children to do it with. She honestly loves being on the trail—as long as she doesn't have to eat beans."

"Well, she'll be eating beans as we continue on. There's no avoiding them. Hopefully there will be some good hunting along the way, though."

"There will. I wish I had the time to hunt as I'd like, but usually by the time we've stopped for the day, all I can really do is see to the animals and take my turn at watch duty."

"I know. Mary's a good hunter, and she usually gets enough for several families." And Trudie was thrilled that her family was now on the list of people who benefited from Mary's hunting skills.

They stopped and looked out over the creek where Trudie and the other women had washed clothes that morning. Joseph turned to Trudie after a short while. "May I kiss you?"

Trudie's heart started beating faster just thinking about it. He'd only kissed her as part of their wedding ceremony, and the idea of kissing him now...well, it both frightened and excited her. "I'd like that."

Joseph was careful not to trap her in his arms, and instead, put his hands lightly on her shoulders. He leaned down and very gently brushed his lips against hers. When she didn't shy away, he tilted his head to one side and deepened the kiss, his tongue tracing her lips before he lifted his head. "Are you all right?"

Trudie felt a little dazed, and she swayed on her feet a bit. "Lovely."

He chuckled. "I won't be afraid to do that again then."

"Why would you be afraid?"

"After what you went through with Mr. Baldwin, I worry that I'll frighten you by kissing you. I don't want to do anything that will make things harder for you."

"I appreciate that."

"You're my wife. It's my duty to protect you from things that frighten you, not become something to fear."

Trudie smiled. "Thank you for feeling that way. I'm sure a lot of men wouldn't mind a whole lot if their wife was afraid."

"I do. I want everything to be comfortable for you." Joseph paused for a moment. "How do you feel about the possibility of a real marriage now?"

"As long as you don't mind taking it slowly, I'm all for it. I think it would be good for me, and I know it would be good for Emily." Trudie wasn't sure if she was really ready to be married to the man for the rest of her life, but she certainly enjoyed his kisses. That had to be a good sign.

"Then we'll keep trying to court whenever we have a chance. Do you want to walk again tomorrow evening?"

She chuckled. "I'll let you know what I feel up to tomorrow. Walking twenty miles per day makes my legs feel like leaves in the fall. They're going to crack with even a little bit of pressure. I haven't heard any of the other women complain, and I'm not going to be the first, but they do hurt."

He laughed. "I think I can understand that. And I like the idea of taking things slowly. It's going to take me a little while to feel like I can handle love again."

She nodded. "I do understand that. I'm really surprised at how quickly Emily has warmed up to me."

"I hope she stays that way and doesn't get too surly as she gets older."

"It's not in her nature to be surly. She's such a good-natured girl."

"You think that because you didn't know her when she was a colicky baby. She had us up all night every night."

"Your wife didn't tend her?"

"Of course, she did," Joseph said. "But she cried loudly enough that I heard every single whimper."

Trudie smiled. "I'm sure she was a delightful baby, even if she was colicky."

"She was. I'm so pleased with your relationship with Emily. The stories you tell her every night make her very happy. I hope you know that."

"I try to make her happy. And I'm teaching her to cook as we go."

"We had a cook stove back in Virginia," he said. "My wife couldn't learn to cook over an open fire for anything. She burned so many things she tried to make."

Trudie shrugged. "I burned a few meals when I first started trying, but I firmly believe if you are a good cook over a stove, you'll also be a good cook over a campfire. You learn to adjust."

"Emily and I are very thankful your mother took the time to teach you as well as she did." Joseph was certainly eating better now that Trudie was the family's cook.

"I am too, to be honest. I was a cook back east for a few years, but first I worked under her. I only went to school until I was ten, because my mother wanted to ensure I was ready to take on a job as a cook. She gave me the best start she knew how." They had reached the edge of camp again, and she sighed, sorry that their day of rest was over. "I'll go get Emily from Margaret, and we'll head back to our wagon."

"And I'll go get the livestock fed and take them down to the water. This is the part of our journey where we really need to ration water."

"Our rain barrel is full. We'll have to keep putting it out to catch the rain anytime it comes along." But they'd been doing that the entire way. It would have to be enough.

He nodded. "I'd rather not use our water rations for the oxen, but if we need to, we will."

"Definitely. I don't want to think about how dirty we'll be before we get to Oregon City. I hope there are some good lakes and rivers along the way."

"There are. The maps I've seen show many rivers and creeks and lakes, but they're going to be a lot more spread out now. We've spoiled ourselves by traveling along the Platte River for so long."

"My legs do not currently *feel* spoiled," she said, stifling a groan. Walking with him had been lovely, but painful as well.

He laughed. "You'll get there. Your legs will be used to it soon, and you'll wonder why they ever hurt to begin with."

"I've never heard any of the women complain about this journey, except maybe Mrs. Mitchell. She calls it a death march." Trudie found herself having a hard time when she walked in a group with Mrs. Mitchell.

"But all of her children are safe, and there are a *lot* of them."

"I just pray it stays that way all the way to our destination. I feel as if we've lost so many." She'd not been close to any of the people who had died, but she'd felt every death just as well. It was difficult knowing you were on a journey where many would not survive.

He nodded. "I do too. Too many." He looked sad for a moment, but then he started off in the direction of the livestock. Every night the men chose where they would keep the livestock for the night. They consoled themselves by realizing the manure left by their oxen would fuel fires later in the summer.

Trudie headed to Margaret's wagon to fetch Emily, who was still playing with the other woman's girls. "Thank you for being willing to keep an eye on Emily for me. We're going to try to take regular walks."

"I think you should!" Margaret said. "Jamie and I are an old married couple now, but we took our turn taking long walks. It's always best to tuck a blanket under your arm as you walk."

Trudie shook her head. "Whatever for?"

"It makes a dalliance a bit easier," Margaret said, winking at her friend.

Trudie blushed. "I...I'll keep that in mind." As she headed back to her own campfire with Emily's hand in hers, the little girl talked about everything she'd done with her friends, which had included making butterflies out of prairie grass.

"It sounds like you had a wonderful time!"

Emily nodded. "I love to play with Annie, Amanda, and Sally. They're my best friends in the whole wide world, and I'll be sad when we reach Oregon and never get to see them again. Is Oregon big? Could we visit?"

Trudie smiled. "We're planning on settling as a community. Most of the people on the wagon train will live close to us." She was thrilled to be able to tell the girl of their future plans because she knew Emily would be happy with them.

Emily let out a little squeal of excitement. "Do you mean it?"

"I do. I've already talked to your papa about it."

"I'm so happy. We will always be friends, and we will be able to go to the same school and visit. When we get to Oregon, will we still be able to go outside and see people? Or will we have to be in the house all the time to be safe?" Emily asked.

Thanks to the discussion she'd had with Joseph on their walk, Trudie understood the question. "There will be dangers in Oregon, but there are dangers everywhere. We will be able to spend time with our friends whenever we would like. I'm even going to be working with Mrs. Prewitt."

"You will?"

"Yes. The two of us plan to open a boarding house with a restaurant. Then people who pass through town will have a place to eat and sleep. And people who live in town can eat there whenever they want to."

"And I'll go to school?" Emily asked.

"I'm not sure if we have a schoolteacher in our group, but I'm certain even if we don't, we can find someone. Do you want to go to school?"

Emily nodded emphatically. "I wasn't old enough before we left, and I don't think Mama would have let me go anyway. She was scared."

"What was she afraid of?" Trudie asked. Emily's mother seemed a little odder every time she was mentioned.

Emily shrugged. "She thought I'd be hurt if I went outside. And she only left when Papa was there."

Trudie sighed. "Well, I'm not afraid of much. We'll make sure you go to school and get to play outside lots."

"I'd like that!" Emily ran ahead to the fire that was slowly going out. "I'm glad you're my new mama."

"You are?" Trudie smiled. "Why's that?"

"Because you care about me, just like I care about you. And you're not scared to go outside and will let me play with my friends."

"In the winter, you'll have to play indoors more than out, but yes. You can always play outside."

Her story for Emily that night was about four little girls who were the best of friends, and the wonderful times they had playing inside during the winter. She hoped that Emily would realize it was always all right for her to have friends to come and play.

Once again, Joseph stood outside the tent and listened, thinking about how wonderful it was that he'd found someone who truly cared about Emily to be her stepmother. He only hoped things would always be as good as they were right then.

EMILY FELL AND TWISTED her ankle the following morning, right after they began their day's walk. Trudie felt around the ankle, but only felt bruising. She finally picked the girl up and put her in the back of the wagon. "Would you like me to ride with you?" she asked, thankful that the wagons moved so slowly it was easy to keep up on foot.

Emily wiped a tear from her eye. "I want my *mama!*"

Trudie closed her eyes for a moment, wishing with all her heart she could make the girl's mother magically appear for her. "I can't do that, but I can ask your papa to come back and sit with you."

Emily shook her head. "No."

Trudie hurried to the front of the wagon and climbed on beside Joseph. It was a little tricky to hold her skirt in one hand and pull herself up into the moving wagon, but she managed. "Emily fell and hurt her ankle. She's crying for her mama."

Joseph frowned. "Where is she now?"

"In the back of the wagon, still crying. I asked her if she wanted you to come sit with her, because I can drive, of course, but she said she only wanted her mama. I do think you should speak with her."

He immediately handed her the leads. "I'll do that."

Trudie took the leads, saying a silent prayer that Joseph would be able to get through to Emily. He knew the girl was hurting, but it would be good for her to have her father beside her.

Joseph was back on the seat beside her less than ten minutes later. It was so much easier to get down and walk than it was to try to climb through all their belongings in the back of the wagon, so that's what he'd done as well. "She wants you to sit with her now."

"What did you say to her?" Trudie didn't want Joseph trying to coerce Emily into wanting her. It had been hard to see the child cry for her mother, but Trudie knew she would have been just the same if she'd lost her mother at such a young age. It was hard enough to lose her when she was an adult.

"I just told her that the reason she has a new mother is for times like this. We'll have the doctor look at her ankle at our noon break, but I think you're right. It's not broken."

Trudie nodded. "All right. I'll go and sit with her then."

"Thank you." He squeezed her hand as he took the leads back from her, and she got down from the wagon to go and see to their daughter.

Chapter Eight

Tuesday, June 23rd, 1852

Emily is getting surly. Her ankle has been sprained and she's not happy having to ride in the wagon. She wants to be walking with her friends.

I had no idea she could be as downright crabby as she's been yesterday and today. I do hope this doesn't continue for long. I know it's hard on her, and I'm doing everything I can to make it more palatable. Hopefully she realizes soon that she doesn't have to be miserable just because she's injured. She's making a choice.

Emily spent the rest of the day in the back of the wagon. Margaret loaned Trudie a children's storybook, and she sat in the back of the wagon with Emily, reading to her. It was a good way to spend the day, but Trudie was sore from the bumps along the trail by the end of the day.

As she cooked supper, Emily sat on the ground beside Trudie, looking terribly dejected until Sally and Amanda came over and sat down with her, telling her everything she'd missed that day. "We wanted you to walk with us," Amanda said, frowning.

"My new mama read me stories in the back of the wagon. I hope I can walk tomorrow." Emily looked positively dejected about having to stay in the back of the wagon. She was not a girl who enjoyed sitting still.

"Did the doctor have to look at it?"

Trudie answered that for the girl. "The doctor was too busy with some sick people to look at it earlier, but he promised to come by before supper tonight and make sure it's not broken."

"Does it hurt to talk?" Sally asked. At three, she was not as sure about most things as her sister and friends.

Emily shook her head. "Just to walk. Trudie carried me and put me in the wagon, and Papa got me out."

Dr. Bentley came by then with Betty at his side. "Now let's look at this ankle." He squatted down beside his young patient. "Which one is it?" he asked. Emily patted her right leg. "Well, let's see what we can see. Did you like riding in the wagon today?"

"I wanted to walk with my friends, but I couldn't."

The doctor carefully examined the ankle. "There's a bit of swelling and bruising, but I think it's just sprained. Is it okay if I wrap something around it so you'll be able to walk some of the day tomorrow?"

Emily nodded. "I would like that. Can I walk all day?"

Dr. Bentley shook his head. "No, I think you should pick the morning or afternoon, and if it starts hurting, you need to let your new mama know about it."

Emily sighed, obviously not happy with his answer. "But if I wake up, and it doesn't hurt?"

"Then you should choose to walk in the morning and not in the afternoon." He finished wrapping her ankle in a long piece of cloth he had with him. "Is it all right if I send Annie over to play with you girls? She talked to me about how much she missed being able to spend the day with you."

"I'd like that. Thank you, doctor."

"You're welcome." The doctor got to his feet and looked over at his wife who was talking animatedly with Trudie. "Are you staying here? Or do you want to go see the other patients with me?"

"I'm going to stay and talk to Trudie. I can learn a lot from watching her cook," Betty answered.

"I'm not sure how much you'll learn from the way I cook venison, but I'm happy to allow you to watch. It's nice to have company on occasion."

"I think it's always nice to have company," Betty said. "I used to hide in the back of our wagon and read, and never get out and even talk to anyone. I'd talk to my sister and no one else. Margaret talked me into spending time with others on the trail, but it wasn't easy for me at first."

"I like Margaret a lot, and I think you know, I'm just learning to talk to people with us as well. It was easier for me to drive and ignore the other women, but if I want to feel like I'm part of the company, then I need to act like it." Trudie smiled. "And Margaret and I have decided to go into business together once we reach our destination. I used to think of it as reaching Oregon, but we're already in Oregon, and we're nowhere close to our final destination."

"No, I suppose we're not." Betty shook her head. "I think in my head we were going to walk for two weeks and be there. Instead, we've been on this trail for over two months, and we're not even close."

"Do you know if everyone is planning on resting in Oregon City once we get there and spending the winter?" Trudie asked. "I've read that's what a lot of folks do, rather than risk the storms that come."

"I don't think so. That's why this company was so eager to move out, even though we knew there would be little fresh grass for the beginning of the journey. The oxen made it through that, though, and now they have beautiful grass to graze on. I think we're only a day or two behind the only company in front of us."

Trudie nodded. "It does seem that we should have passed them by now with as consistent as we've been about moving so much every day. The thing with the former captain slowed us way down, but I think we're all glad to see he wasn't the heartless coward we assumed him to be."

"Heartless coward. I like that!" Betty grinned at Trudie. "He's giving poor Mrs. Gabriel a run for her money. She feels like she needs to care for him because he was hurt saving her daughter."

"I spelled her one afternoon, and I swear she should be nominated for sainthood." Trudie took the meat off the fire, and quickly mixed together a gravy in the drippings from the meat.

"I agree." Betty carefully watched Trudie. "I've never seen anyone mix the water and flour in another bowl before adding it. My mother always mixed flour with the drippings."

"I do that some too, but I like the way it turns out this way a little better." Trudie shrugged. "My mother taught me the way your mother taught you. I just experimented with different ways, and this seems to work best for me."

"Maybe I'll do some experimenting as well." Betty smiled. "I like to learn new things."

"I do as well. I'll make a cake with some of the dried fruit we have for dessert to help cheer Emily up. She is not a fan of having to ride in the back of the wagon." Trudie looked over at the girl who was now smiling with her friends. Emily couldn't be horribly hurt with as happy as she looked at that moment, which was a relief to Trudie.

Betty left as soon as she'd watched Trudie whip up her dessert, committing what Trudie put in it to memory. "I'll try it as well. It's hard to keep my family happy with the meals I have available to cook."

Trudie sighed. "Cooking is an art form, and like any other, if you don't have the best tools at hand, it's more difficult, but it can still be done and done well."

As Betty walked away Trudie carefully put the cake on to bake. She knew it would make Emily happy, and she truly hoped it would please Joseph, which was odd to her, because she had never cared about pleasing him, but suddenly she did. She was taking better care with her appearance as well—as best she could—wanting to please him physically.

As soon as he walked into camp, she served their plates, sending the little girls back to their families so they could eat as well. "Is this the last of the venison?" Joseph asked. "I may take my rifle on our walk tonight. It would be nice if I could be the one supplying meat to others for a change."

"I think that's a wonderful idea." But then Trudie's eyes went to Emily. "I'll need to stay here, though. Emily can't really play with her friend."

"Nonsense," he said. "She'll go to Mrs. Prewitt's and play with her girls as she's been doing. They'll just have to play differently like they were here tonight."

"I'm sure that would be fine if Emily wouldn't mind. Emily?" Trudie asked.

Emily nodded, excitement filling her face. "I'd like that very much."

"I'll carry you over after I do the dishes then," Trudie said. With all the carrying of the child she'd done that day, Trudie was thankful for her time driving. Her arms were much stronger than they'd been just months before.

After supper, Joseph found his rifle, while Trudie carried Emily to Margaret's wagon. "Do you mind watching her again? I know you said yesterday you didn't mind, but today she's injured."

Margaret shook her head. "Of course, I don't mind. I have a game in mind to teach the girls that will allow them to sit and play instead of running around like heathens."

Trudie laughed. "They do rather seem like heathens at times, don't they?"

Joseph walked up behind her then. "Who seems like heathens?"

"The little girls who run around with Emily. They are wild little things when they get to playing," Margaret said. "Including my own two girls, of course."

"Of course," Joseph said with a smile. "Well, I hope they all have fun sitting quietly tonight."

"I'll make sure of it," Margaret said.

"And when we get back, the cake will have cooled enough to eat," Trudie said with a smile.

"That will be nice," Emily said. "Now go so I can play with my friends."

Joseph nodded. "Yes, ma'am."

As they walked away, Joseph slung the gun over one shoulder, but he still held Trudie's hand.

"I'm sorry I let her get hurt today," Trudie said. "I've felt badly about it all day."

"Why would you feel badly? She runs around like a heathen! You and Margaret were right about that."

"I know, but I've only been a mother for a week, and here I am, injuring the child I've been given to protect from harm."

Joseph shook his head. "You didn't injure her. She injured herself by acting like a wild child."

Trudie felt a corner of her mouth lift up. "You're truly not angry with me about it?"

"Not at all. If you'd pushed her or hit her and injured her, it would be different, but you were completely innocent." Joseph hated that she even felt like she needed to apologize for the girl getting hurt. "So how was your day in the back of the wagon?"

She sighed. "Long. And Emily was so miserable. I hate that she had to sit there the whole day. I read to her, but she kept trying to see what her friends were doing outside, and she couldn't even concentrate on what I was saying. The doctor said it's not broken, and he wants her to ride half the day tomorrow."

"I'm glad sitting with her isn't my duty." He shook his head. "I love my daughter, but she's perfectly dreadful when she can't do what she wants to do."

"She's a very sweet girl," Trudie said. "But she was difficult today. She wanted to be down running with her friends."

"And I'm sure she told you that over and over."

"She did. I was just glad that after you talked to her, she quit asking for her mama. I felt so bad when she was doing that. I know I can substitute in many things but wanting to be held by your real mother when you're injured is just not one of those things."

"It'll be different soon. She does love you, and she'll get used to the idea of going to you when something happens. It's perfectly natural."

Trudie nodded. "I do hope you're right."

"Shh…" Joseph stopped walking and dropped her hand, bringing his rifle to his shoulder. With two shots, he brought down two deer. When they were sure there weren't any more, he smiled at her. "Run to camp and get me some help toting these back. We'll be able to share the meat with others this time."

"I'm on my way!" Trudie hurried back, though she didn't full-out run. The first person she encountered was Mr. Prewitt, and she said, "Joseph just brought down two deer, a doe and a buck. Can you help him bring them back to camp? We'll happily share the meat."

"I'd be happy to help. That way?" he pointed in the direction she'd come from, and when she nodded, he took off at a run.

She asked two more men for help, and when they all left, she joined Margaret at her camp, noting that the girls were sitting on a blanket on the ground and three of them had their eyes closed. Emily was telling them something.

"Is this the new game you told me about?" Trudie asked Margaret.

"Yes it is, but what are you doing back so soon?" Margaret asked.

"Joseph shot two deer, and he needed help getting them back to camp."

Margaret's eyes lit up. "Oh, that's wonderful. You've been blessed with fresh meat!"

"As have you. Don't think we won't share with as often as others have shared with us."

"I feel like we've all been blessed to be part of such a wonderful group of people. If you have to walk two-thousand miles, it's always good to do it with people you care for."

Trudie smiled. "I'm surprised anyone is considering me one of the people they care about, but I'm happy you do."

"Of course, I do. Soon, we'll be running a business together, and our girls will play together every day. You need to hurry up and have a baby as well. We could have more children playing together." Margaret seemed to like the idea of raising their children together.

Unsure how to respond to that, Trudie changed the subject. "Tell me about this game you have the girls playing."

Margaret grinned. "Not ready to talk about that. I remember being a newlywed for the first time. The game is simple. They take turns describing something they can see, but they can't use the name. The ones with their eyes closed have to guess what it is the person who has them open is describing. Then when someone guesses, the play moves to the next girl. I came up with it during the long hours of driving before I married Jamie. I thought it would be good to have it ready for the girls to play if one of them was sick or injured while we were on the trail."

"And instead, you had them play it when my girl was injured. Thank you for taking care of her."

"Always. I'm happy to have her play with my girls anytime. I know you and your new husband need some time to get to know one another better. It's hard to marry again when you've lost someone you love."

"I worry Joseph will never stop loving Emily's mother, which I could understand, but I find I want a little of his love as well."

"You already have Emily's. There's no doubt about that. And I've noticed that your husband is looking at you differently these past few days. I'm sure it's because he's starting to care for you." Margaret smiled at her. "He's a good man."

"He is. Better than I realized for certain."

When the men got back to camp with the deer, Trudie carried Emily back to camp, and served up six slices of the cake, sharing a piece with each of the men who had helped with the meat. "I so appreciate all of your help."

Mr. Prewitt shook his head. "You don't have to do this. Your husband has already promised he'll share some of his meat. We don't need cake as well."

"You get both," Trudie said with a smile. "Then you'll remember us when you get meat, and we don't."

The men laughed at that. "We'll always remember that you were kind and shared your kill with us, and we'll do the same for you," Mr. Prewitt said.

"I thank you for your generosity and kind spirit," Trudie said.

"And I thank *you* for cake, Trudie!" Emily said.

Trudie grinned at her new daughter. "I made it so you would feel better after your injury today. Did it work?"

"Yes!" Emily took another bite.

After the men had hung the deer upside down to drain the blood from them, they all promised to be at their camp before dawn to help butcher the meat and share it among them and others in the camp who had shared before. It was becoming a way of life, this sharing with others who were also in need of good food.

The meat had been butchered and distributed before Trudie had breakfast ready the following morning. When Joseph joined her and Emily for the meal, Trudie sighed happily. "It's nice to be the ones to have meat to share for a change. I always hated accepting from the others when we hadn't yet reciprocated, but now we have."

"And we'll continue to do so as we can."

Emily sighed happily looking at her plate. "Johnny cakes and honey. Trudie, you are the best second mama in the whole world! Especially if you let me walk all day. I feel fine now!"

"The doctor said you may walk half the day. No more. And if it starts hurting a lot again, we'll make sure you rest even more than that."

"It's not going to hurt. I promise!" Emily said. "I'll do fine walking. You'll see!"

"I hope you will! But if not, we'll ride for a little while. I bet your papa would even let you ride up front for a while if you wanted."

"I would." Joseph smiled at his daughter. "You can ride wherever you want, but I don't want your ankle to get worse and not heal properly just because you wanted to walk with your friends."

Emily sighed. "Yes, Papa."

Trudie grinned. It was so obvious Emily didn't want to have to ride, but she'd do as she was told. For now.

Chapter Nine

Wednesday, June 24th, 1852

It stormed today. There was thunder, lightning, and it just poured down on us. I thought it was thrilling to watch from the back of the wagon, but little Emily was afraid. I wish I'd had the right words for her, so she'd know everything would be all right. If I were her real mother, I'm certain I would have known what to say immediately.

We were only able to move half the usual distance today. The rainstorm forced us to stop. Filling our rain barrels is a priority at this point because we're no longer traveling along a river. I pray there is more rain to keep our barrels full as we continue on this journey. Joseph has told me there will be other streams and rivers along our path, but it seems so dry here. I hope he is right.

Emily was hurting within an hour of starting the day, and she went to Trudie crying. "I don't want to ride, but my ankle hurts again."

Trudie sighed. "I have an idea. I'm going to put you in the back of the wagon, but then I'm going to see if I can make a little magic happened for my enchanted princess." She hated that the little girl was hurting, but it was even worse that she felt isolated. She hoped she could easily fix that.

Her face showing her pain, Emily nodded. "I don't want to be hurt."

"I know you don't, baby."

Edna walked toward them. "She's *not* a baby, you know."

"I know. But she's hurt."

"Would some of my peppermint stick help?"

Trudie shook her head. She didn't know if licking the nasty thing would help or not, but she felt like Edna should keep the germs that went with her peppermint stick to herself. "No, she just needs to rest her ankle." Trudie lifted Emily in her arms and carried her to the back of the wagon, setting her inside. "I'll be right back."

Emily wiped at the tears with the back of her arm. "Hurry."

"I will." Trudie went to both Margaret and Betty, asking a simple question. "Would you mind if the girls rode in the back of the wagon with Emily? She's sad that she hurts too much to walk, but I think her day would be much better if the other girls joined her."

Margaret's face lit up and she nodded. "If that will help, then I think that's what you should do. What a good idea."

Trudie gathered the three girls together, and they all climbed into the back of the wagon with Emily. Emily's face when her friends joined her was absolutely priceless. She was obviously ready to have fun with her friends. "Did your mamas say you could ride with me?" Emily asked.

Trudie nodded. "All three of them will ride with you until the noon meal, and then you'll nap after. By the time your nap is over, you may be able to walk for a little while again."

"Oh, thank you, Mama!" Emily's voice was filled with excitement. She wouldn't have to ride alone.

Trudie's heart felt like it swelled a dozen sizes larger at Emily's calling her Mama. It just felt right. "I'll check on you all in a little while."

Joseph heard his daughter's exclamation and he frowned. He wasn't sure if he was ready for Emily to call Trudie Mama. Her mother hadn't been gone for long enough to be replaced.

When Trudie climbed onto the front of the wagon to talk to him, Joseph wanted to tell her to stay away from his child. Their relationship had thrilled him the day before, but today...well, today it only angered him. She couldn't claim his late wife's life, even if they were married.

"Emily's in the back of the wagon again, but she has three friends with her this time. Her ankle was starting to swell, and she was devastated she couldn't walk any longer." Trudie shook her head. "I felt bad for her."

"Thank you for taking good care of *my* daughter." He didn't mean to place the emphasis on the word my, but it was there nonetheless.

Trudie glanced at him, wondering if there was a problem she didn't know about. Instead of asking and being overheard by four little girls, she simply said, "I'll return to the women."

He nodded, staring straight ahead. There was something wrong between them. Trudie could feel it, but she had no idea what it could possibly be. Everything was fine that morning before they began their day's journey.

Trudie jumped down, but instead of joining the women, she walked off to one side, her mind going over and over what had just happened with Joseph. His tone had been so cold, she felt like she could have frozen her hand on it.

By their noon break, Trudie had come to the conclusion that he didn't want her around Emily because she was a murderess. What else could it possibly be that would make him talk to her as if she was the stranger she'd been a couple of weeks before? Now that they'd shared a real kiss, it seemed like they should just be growing closer.

Penelope walked over to join Trudie. "Are you all right?"

Trudie nodded. "Yes, of course. Just needed to be alone with my thoughts for a while."

"Do you want to talk about whatever is bothering you?"

For a moment—but just a moment—Trudie considered pouring her heart out to Penelope and explaining the entire situation. But she couldn't see the hatred that would certainly be in the other woman's eyes. No one would want to be friends or start a business with a murderess, and she didn't trust anyone enough to let them know her secret.

"No but thank you. I think I just need to have a little time of contemplation."

Penelope reached down and squeezed Trudie's hand. "I'll be walking with the others if you change your mind."

Trudie nodded, but she kept staring straight ahead. She hated that Joseph now realized she was a terrible person and not fit to be around his daughter, but who could blame him? Emily was a precious child, and Joseph was protecting her as any good father would.

When they stopped for the noon meal, Joseph was just as cold as he'd been in the wagon that morning. He thanked her for the meal but spoke only when he needed to speak. Trudie couldn't help but sink into silence and despair beside him. Her whole life had changed because of one awful moment months before. Never again would a man think she was fit to be a wife or a mother. Never.

Trudie checked Emily's ankle before using a bit of their precious water to wash the dishes. "It looks like the swelling is going down from this morning. You may walk after your nap if you feel up to it."

"I'll decide what my daughter can do or not do." Joseph looked at Emily's ankle. "You may walk if you choose."

"Thanks, Papa," Emily said, looking confused. Trudie knew that what was going on between her papa and her new mother had to be confusing.

She only wished there was something she could say to Emily to explain it all, but there wasn't. Nothing at all. She couldn't ever let the little girl know she was a murderess.

Trudie made a huge pot of the venison cut into chunks and rice that night with a little bit of gravy to make it all moist. Emily loved it and talked about how wonderful it was for a good portion of the meal.

"Am I going to play with my friends while you walk?" Emily asked.

Trudie glanced at Joseph, who shook his head. "We're not going to walk tonight. I have to check on the livestock."

Emily looked confused, but she said nothing.

Trudie felt his words cut through her like a knife. Why had he changed his mind about her so suddenly? It made no sense to her. No sense at all.

"Emily, we should make some biscuits with honey tonight. Did your mama teach you to make biscuits over a fire?" Trudie was aware that Joseph got up then and stomped away from camp, but it made no sense to her, so she continued talking to the child. "I actually prefer how biscuits taste over a campfire to cooked on a stove." The last thing she said may have been a stretch, but Trudie did like biscuits cooked over a campfire.

Emily shook her head. "No, when Mama tried to bake biscuits over a campfire, she always burned them."

"I see," Trudie said. "Well, let's learn to do it tonight, since you are hurt anyway, and you can't really play with your friends."

"Trudie?" Emily asked.

"Yes?"

"What is wrong with Papa?"

Trudie shrugged. "I'm not sure. I do hope he feels better tomorrow, though."

By the time Joseph was back at camp, it was dark, and the dishes had long since been washed and the biscuits packed away for breakfast in the morning. He stood for a moment, listening for one of Trudie's bedtime stories, but he heard nothing, so he climbed under the wagon. He wished he'd done anything but marry so quickly after his dear wife's death. She would have hated knowing her daughter was calling another woman Mama so soon.

JOSEPH'S MOOD WAS JUST as foul the following day as it had been. Trudie felt that she understood why he was angry with her, so she didn't ask him about it. Instead, she took care of her chores, and went about her business as she normally would.

She made a white gravy with pieces of bacon cut up in it for their breakfast and poured it over the biscuits. It was a filling meal, and she knew it was a welcome change from many of the things she made. It was strange that she was a well-practiced cook, but there were very few things that were available for her to make on the trail.

There was some of the venison and rice left from the night before, and Trudie planned to serve that for the noon meal, but she had no idea what to do for her supper. Perhaps beans again, if no meat became available for her to use.

Joseph kissed Emily on her forehead before going to hitch up the wagon, leaving Trudie to decide whether Emily's ankle would support her for walking a portion of the day. It was strange that he'd felt so strongly about making the decision the day before, but today he didn't even look at the injury. It just showed her that he didn't want her having much to do with Emily. They certainly wouldn't be able to stay married after they reached their destination, but maybe that was for the best. He knew her secret. Without him, she could easily separate from the others and open a boarding house on her own.

Emily's ankle looked like the swelling was gone and the bruising around the bone was starting to fade. "I think you can walk for a while today unless it starts paining you," Trudie said.

"I'll like that. Thank you, Trudie."

Trudie was sad that the girl had only called her Mama the one time, but it made sense. She'd needed friends to play with and she'd been excited. The word had obviously simply slipped out.

Trudie walked with the other women again that day, but she mostly listened to their chatter, instead of actually being part of the conversation. She had to pull back and not become close to these women, knowing she wouldn't be able to stay with them. No, they knew she'd married Joseph, and she wasn't going to be able to explain why they were suddenly apart once they arrived.

Emily was able to make it all morning, and when Trudie checked her ankle after the noon meal, it looked the same as it had that morning. "I think you can keep walking," Trudie said softly, worried that Joseph would jump in, but he remained silent.

Emily clapped her hands. "I can walk all afternoon!"

"After your nap, you can walk," Trudie corrected.

"That's all right. My friends nap when I do, so we'll still be able to play a lot!"

"Enjoy yourself, because we're probably going to have beans for supper."

Emily groaned. "Anything but beans. Please!"

Trudie frowned. "I can make a gravy from our jerky and serve it with potatoes and carrots if you want."

"Yes, please!"

"Don't be spoiling my daughter," Joseph said harshly. "She can eat beans if that's the best thing for you to cook."

Trudie bit her lip. "It's not really the *best* thing, but we'll be eating a lot of beans toward the end of our journey if we don't work them into our meals now."

"Then we'll have beans tonight, and Emily will be thankful she has food to eat." Joseph put his bowl down and strode from the campsite. Trudie watched him leave, wondering how she could make the meal more palatable for Emily without angering her husband—more than he was already angry that was.

Emily sat staring after her father. "Why is he angry with us?"

"I don't know, sweetheart. I really don't." Trudie sighed. "Would you like to make biscuits again tonight? I can show you how to make them and fry up a few pieces of bacon we can eat on the biscuits."

Emily smiled for a moment, but then it faded. "That would make Papa angry. We need to be nice to him and do as we should."

"Then that's what we'll do," Trudie said. "But I'll make a cake for dessert, and he can't stop us from that, can he?"

Emily giggled. "I'll help make the cake!"

"Good. It's a plan." Trudie knew Joseph was angry with her, but she didn't like it that he was taking his anger out on the child.

As she walked with the other women that afternoon, Trudie was lost in thought. For a short while, it had seemed she and Joseph were going to be able to make things work out between them. But now...now that she knew she loved him, he was drifting away quickly. She would simply have to keep her chin up, though, because things didn't seem like they were going to change. For whatever reason, Joseph was too angry with her for that.

Her life had changed so much in a few short months. She'd had her life spread out in front of her, and she'd felt like she could do anything, but then after Mr. Baldwin had acted so horribly, she'd felt as if she would always be alone, looking over her shoulder. The further they'd come on the trail, the safer she had felt, and then she'd married Joseph, and little Emily had been the only light she'd needed to see her way.

And then she'd begun to believe she could actually find love with a man who knew all about her past. Now...she was devastated again. She was going to have to spend the rest of her life alone. She only wished she'd never told Joseph the truth. Because it had surely pushed him away.

"What do you think, Trudie?" Penelope asked.

Trudie blinked a couple of times, pulled from her thoughts. "About what? I was woolgathering, I'm afraid."

The other women laughed. "That's what you're supposed to do when you're a newlywed," Hannah said softly.

"What do you think about all of us making a big meal together on Saturday night? And then we'd eat as a group. I've heard many companies do that every night, but ours never really has." Penelope grinned, but she didn't join in the laughter of the other women.

"That sounds lovely," Trudie said, caring little about what would happen in three days. She was too worried about getting through *that* day while facing her husband's anger.

"Oh, good!" Margaret smiled at her. "Jamie had some of your cake the other night, and I thought it would be nice if you'd be willing to make a few cakes for everyone."

Trudie smiled, but it felt forced. "I'd enjoy that. I've been working with Emily on baking. Are we cooking for the entire camp?"

Margaret nodded. "That's the idea. We'll make a meal for all the camp before we come together and dance and enjoy music as a group. I think it will make us all feel more united. Though now that I think about it, I wonder if Sunday afternoon might be better. It would feel like a church potluck from back home."

Trudie nodded. "I think Sunday would be better. I'd be happy to do my laundry the night before, so we'd all have a little more time to cook on Sunday."

The women all agreed that Sunday was better.

When lightning lit the sky then, they all saw the dark clouds forming. "At least we're not near a river this time," Trudie said. "But we're going to be awfully wet soon. I wonder if the men will stop so we can set the rain barrels out. I feel like half of my water supply is already gone, and we need that water for cooking."

The wagons all seemed to stop rolling at her command. Trudie went to her wagon and half rolled and half lifted the rain barrel to the ground, prying the lid off so it could fill up with the precious water they needed for their journey.

The men all unhitched the oxen and led them to a free spot. The entire camp was moving about all at once, and Emily woke in the back of the wagon and looked at Trudie. "What's happening?"

"There's a rainstorm. We're going to collect the rain in our barrels."

"Are we camping here tonight?" Emily asked, rubbing her eyes.

"I'm not certain. I haven't heard what the captains have decided about that yet."

Trudie didn't mind the good washing that the rain gave her, but when the lightning grew closer, she knew she didn't want to be out in it. There was too much danger involved. Climbing into the back of the wagon with Emily, she sat shivering slightly, until Emily found one of the blankets. "I don't like the rain out here. It was nice at home, but we don't have a house to go into." Emily sighed. "Mama was afraid of rain back home, but I was brave and took care of her."

"No, we don't have a house, but we can still take care of each other," Trudie said. "It'll be all right. We're just going to sit and watch it rain."

"Would you tell me another story about Emily and her friends?"

Trudie laughed. "I'd love to tell you another story. This story is about how true friends never forsake each other."

Chapter Ten

Thursday, June 25th, 1852

The captains decided that there was no point moving on from camp today because the mud would keep us from being able to move well anyway. Instead, we stayed in, and the men shot four buffalo that were evenly split among the different families. I feel blessed to have received both fresh and dried meat. All of the women dried the buffalo together, and we had a lovely time doing it.

We lost Mr. Davies today. His horse bucked while the men were chasing the buffalo, and he was thrown off, only to be trampled by the buffalo. Mrs. Davies was a schoolteacher before their marriage, and they have no children. I hope she will be willing to settle near the rest of us and teach our children.

While in camp, Joseph took an extra shift watching out and I cleaned out the wagon. I found some things that will be a blessing for our trip west. It was a nice day of respite, but we've had many of late. I worry that we won't reach our final destination until it is too late in the year to move comfortably, but that's why our company moved out so early. We wanted to avoid the snows.

I pray that still happens, and we lose no one else along the way.

The rain stopped by supper time, but they had all collected a good amount of water in their rain barrels. It had been a hard rain for the time it had lasted. The captains were still trying to decide if they would be able to move on the following day with the mud that would be left behind.

Trudie made the beans Joseph had told her to make, but she and Emily had a cake baking on the fire as well when it was time to eat. Joseph looked at the fire, and then seemed to look right through Trudie. As much as she hated it, Trudie knew that he would never forgive her for her past...or her present. He found her lacking. She would have to learn to be alone again once they reached Oregon City.

After the dishes were finished, Emily asked if she could play with her friends, and Joseph conceded. Trudie took some mending out of the wagon. She'd stepped on the hem of one of her dresses helping Emily, and it had torn. She was seriously considering putting a shorter temporary hem into the dress that she would take out once they had reached Oregon City. It was too hard to face the conditions of the trail with her dress dragging the ground the way it did. She wished she was brave enough to make herself a split skirt like Mary wore, but she knew it wasn't a good idea. If Joseph disapproved of her now, she could only imagine how he would feel if she ran around dressed in a split skirt!

As she sat and sewed, Joseph pulled out a piece of wood and a knife, and he began painstakingly carving the wood. He didn't speak, but she didn't need him to. She already understood that he wanted nothing else to do with her for the rest of her life. She'd do all she could to take care of Emily, but she wouldn't let herself be hurt by him again.

She poured herself a cup of coffee and offered him one.

"No, thank you," he answered, not looking at her. Looking at her made him want things he shouldn't want. His real wife—Emily's mother—lay miles and miles behind them on the trail, where the wagons had driven over her resting place to keep from being found by wolves. He couldn't be choosing another woman to love already. It wasn't right.

"We'll have cake before bedtime," she said softly, and then she continued her stitching. There was no reason to try to converse with a man who had no desire to even look at her. She'd really thought he could accept what she'd done, but obviously he couldn't.

When Emily came back to camp, they had exchanged no more words. The silence felt deafening, but Trudie was too stubborn to try to talk to him. Not after the way he'd been treating her.

"Is it time for cake, Trudie? Mrs. Prewitt said the girls had to go to bed."

"And you'll be going to bed soon too," Trudie said. "But yes, it's time for cake."

Emily clapped her hands. "I love cake!"

Trudie laughed. "I couldn't tell. I'm so glad you told me!"

Together, Trudie and Emily cut three pieces of the cake and served it. Emily took the piece to her papa. "I helped make it, Papa!"

"Then I'm sure it's delicious. Thank you." Joseph took a bite of the cake and smiled at his daughter. She was learning so much more from Trudie than she'd been able to learn from her mother, but just thinking about that made his heart sink. He should be loyal and true, and instead he'd fallen in love with another woman.

As they ate the cake, Emily told her father about how frightened she'd been in the back of the wagon while the rain had fallen.

Joseph shook his head. "You were never afraid of the thunder back home. Why are you scared now?"

"We have no house here. Just a wagon. In a house, you're safe." Emily's words were simple, and Joseph sighed.

"I wish I could take your fears away."

Emily sighed. "So do I."

When they went to bed a short while later, Trudie's story for Emily was about being afraid but being courageous enough to get through her fears.

Emily smiled. "Were you afraid when you were a little girl?"

"All the time," Trudie said. "I lost my papa when I was much younger than you, and it was just my mama and me. We lived in her employers house, and I was always afraid they'd make us go away."

"Why?" Emily asked.

"I heard people yell at children, and I was afraid if I got too loud, they wouldn't want my mama to work there anymore. It was a silly fear. And I was afraid of thunder. Because my mama worked so much, she couldn't sit with me and talk to me during the storms."

"That's sad." Emily sighed. "I miss my mama, but I have you now."

Joseph had been about to go into the tent when he heard Emily's word. He froze, shaking his head. He'd really messed up by giving into Emily's wishes and marrying Trudie so soon. His late wife deserved more love than she was being given. So much more.

THEY HAD TO STAY OVER the next day because of how muddy it was, and Emily was thrilled to have a non-church day to just play with her friends. The children couldn't even pick up manure because the ground was so wet. Thankfully, they had a good supply, and they could easily find more the following days.

Joseph took an extra watch that day because it was easier than spending the day with his wife, and he found himself with Mr. Hastings, who had recently married the Mitchell's oldest girl, Mary. Joseph talked little, but Bob spoke of how much he loved his wife often. It seemed an odd arrangement to Joseph because Mary was better with a gun than she was at cooking.

Back at the wagon, Trudie spent the day going through everything they owned, so she could pare things down. There were two flour sacks that she easily combined, and she found eggs in the barrel of cornmeal Joseph had brought. She'd heard of packing eggs that way and them staying fresh the entire way, but she hadn't heard it until they were already on their journey. She would make good use of the eggs she'd found.

As she was finishing, she found a journal. She was certain it was a recording of the journey, but it hadn't been made by her, so she didn't feel as if it was her right to read it. Instead, she tucked it aside and planned to give it to Joseph as soon as he returned.

Shortly after the noon meal—which Joseph had missed during his time on watch—Trudie heard a great rumbling. Looking out, she saw an entire herd of buffalo running not far from camp.

Everyone was on alert, and many of the men jumped on horseback with their rifles to try to get meat for the entire camp. The more they could kill as a group, the more food they would have, both dried meat and fresh.

The hunters were gone, and without Joseph there to protest, Trudie sent Emily out to play with her friends while she did the dishes on her own. There was a meal left for Joseph when he returned, but she had a feeling he was trying to shoot a buffalo as well. He was on the end of the camp where she'd seen the buffalo.

A few hours later, there was much rejoicing in camp. Between them, the men had killed four buffalo. They were brought back to camp in chunks, as the horses were unable to carry the buffalo *and* the men.

Together the women worked on the meat for the rest of the day, drying it and each taking some for their family's supper that night.

Mary seemed unhappy because the men hadn't allowed her to hunt with them. If Mary's husband had been there, Trudie had no doubt that Mary would have been invited, but since it was left up to the men who were in camp, she was told to stay.

Trudie was thrilled not to have to serve beans to Emily and Joseph that night, and she instead, made a roast, and she made up a meat pie to cook the following night from what was left of the fresh meat. When the dishes were done and Emily was off playing with her friends, Trudie gave Joseph the journal. "I'm not certain who has been writing in this, but I found it in the wagon when I was sorting through everything earlier. I thought you'd want it."

Joseph stared at the object in his hand. When they'd left Virginia, his wife, Alice, had begun writing in the journal every morning. "Thank you." What else could he say? He now wanted this memory of the woman he'd loved for so long. Perhaps she hadn't been as courageous as Trudie was, but she was a good wife and a very good mother.

He walked away from the camp with the journal in his hand, thankful that it was still light so late in the day. It made it possible to read his first wife's words.

He expected a simple journal of how far they'd gone each day, but instead he found himself reading his late wife's innermost thoughts and feelings about the journey they made. Each page was filled with so much emotion.

It was the journal entry she wrote the day before they left Independence that struck his heart the most.

March 28th, 1852

We leave Missouri tomorrow for our trek to Oregon. It will be a long, difficult journey from what I've heard and read, and I fear I will not make it the whole way. No, I say that wrong. I feel with everything inside me that I will not make it to Oregon.

I love my family, and I know I will be leaving them. I pray that in twenty years I read these words I've written and see that I was wrong, but I fear it will be the opposite. Someone else will be reading these words long in the future. Perhaps it will even be my precious Emily, who has made my life worth living for so long.

I do not know why I am given to so many fears and bouts of melancholy, but I do know that without Emily, I would not have survived as long as I have. I pray that Joseph will realize after my death that he must marry soon and find a new mother for my sweet daughter. With as special as she is, she cannot raise herself, and there must be a good firm hand to guide her in all things.

It would be nice if that woman were able to cook, so she could teach my daughter what I cannot, but more than anything, I want Joseph to marry someone that will look upon Emily as her own daughter, and who will care for her the same way I would have. No matter what, Emily's needs must always come first.

And now, I must stop writing for we leave at first light, and I will not be the one to keep the company from moving on. Though I'm certain I will not feel as if I can make friends as we go, Emily will. She is a gregarious child who is filled with love and doesn't have the kinds of fears I have. With God's grace, that will never change.

Joseph read the words over and over, wondering how Emily's mother had known she wouldn't survive the journey. There were other pages filled with how much she didn't want to go. How afraid she was to go. Joseph had realized she wasn't always happy, but he didn't realize that she had been so fearful or filled with melancholy. Perhaps it was meant that she didn't live longer.

He took a deep breath and said a prayer that Alice would rest in peace and she would realize that her greatest wish had been fulfilled.

He'd married a woman who could not only cook, but who loved Emily as much as she would have loved her own child.

He closed the journal, promising himself he'd read more, but right then, he needed to talk to his new wife, and explain why he'd been acting so strangely. Trudie had a right to know everything.

He hurried back to camp and found his wife still sitting at the fire with his daughter. Trudie was sewing and sweet Emily was talking. A lot. Joseph wondered at Trudie's ability to simply sit and let Emily talk, but she never seemed to grow tired of listening to the child.

"Would you walk with me, Trudie?" he asked.

Trudie looked at him, seeming to be shocked by his words. "It's almost time to put Emily to bed."

"Emily can put herself to bed tonight. I need to talk to you."

"Let me ask Mrs. Mitchell to keep an ear out for her." Trudie walked to the next wagon over where she told Mary's mother that she was going to go on a short walk with Joseph.

Mrs. Mitchell simply smiled. "I don't mind listening for her. I can even sit with her until she falls asleep."

"I think she'll be fine," Trudie said before joining her husband, who was carefully putting the journal she'd given him in the back of the wagon.

He took her hand in his and led her out of the camp. "I need to apologize to you," he said softly.

"Why?" Trudie wasn't certain she understood why he was acting so differently all of a sudden.

"On Tuesday, I heard Emily call you Mama, and it made me feel as if I'd done something wrong. I felt like we hadn't taken an appropriate amount of time to mourn Alice, and it filled me with guilt. Emily shouldn't have been calling you Mama nearly so fast, and I shouldn't have been thinking about having a real marriage with you. And I certainly shouldn't have fallen in love with you." He paused and stopped walking once they were a good distance from the camp. "But that journal...I read over part of it. The day before we left Independence, she made an entry into it that talked about how she was certain she wouldn't make it all the way to Oregon."

"She did?" Trudie still wasn't sure what all this meant, and she hoped he'd tell her quickly. She wasn't an overly patient woman.

"And she wrote that she hoped that I would marry quickly, so Emily could grow up with a mother who loved her." He shook his head. "Until reading her words, I hadn't realized that her entire life was ruled by fear and melancholy. She was desperately afraid of making this journey, but I insisted. And I always felt like it killed her. I think she simply allowed herself to die. She wouldn't drink coffee. She drank it all the time at home, but she didn't want to drink it once we were on the trail. I kept telling her that the doctor said she could keep the sickness at bay if she drank coffee instead. She said she'd lost her taste for it, and only wanted to drink water."

"Do you think she died deliberately?" she asked.

"I do. And I think she would be very happy to know that I married you and that you love Emily as much as you would love your own."

"I thought you were avoiding me because you knew I was a murderess."

He shook his head. "You are *not* a murderess. What you did was in self-defense. No one would accuse you of murdering, because you never planned to do it, and you have so much remorse for what happened accidentally. "No, I was avoiding you because I was falling in love with you, and I felt like I was betraying Alice's memory."

"You *were* falling in love with me?"

"I was. I'm not any longer, because I *am* in love with you." Joseph sighed. "I'm so sorry to make you feel unwanted this week, and I know that's just what I did. I felt so guilty. Now, I know that Alice would have wanted me to marry you, and my heart feels lighter. I love you, Trudie Simmons."

Trudie threw her arms around him. "And I love you, Joseph. So much. And Emily. I couldn't love Emily any more if she'd grown inside me."

"I know that. And it's why you're the new wife and mother Emily and I needed to complete our little family. Now, we'll still take things slowly as to the physical part of our marriage, but I want you to know, as soon as you're ready, I am."

She smiled. "I appreciate the extra time. I do love it when you touch me, and the fear hasn't come back yet, but I'm afraid it will."

"As I said, we'll take it as slowly as you need to." He pulled her closer and kissed her softly. "Just knowing that you love me the way I love you makes it so much easier to wait. We're staying a family, whether we settle with the rest of the company or not."

"I do want to settle with everyone. Mrs. Prewitt and I are making business plans."

He smiled. "Good. I want to hear everything about them. You'll walk with me tomorrow evening?"

Trudie rested her head on his shoulder as they walked back toward camp. "I will walk with you every evening for the rest of my life."